About the Author

Bruna Porto was born and raised in Brazil, and showed a passion for books from a very young age. Now residing in Canada, Bruna introduces *Sea of Butterflies* as her debut work in the English language.

Sea of Butterflies

Bruna Porto

Sea of Butterflies

Olympia Publishers
London

www.olympiapublishers.com
OLYMPIA PAPERBACK EDITION

Copyright © Bruna Porto 2024

The right of Bruna Porto to be identified as author of
this work has been asserted in accordance with sections 77 and 78 of
the Copyright, Designs and Patents Act 1988.

All Rights Reserved

No reproduction, copy or transmission of this publication
may be made without written permission.
No paragraph of this publication may be reproduced,
copied or transmitted save with the written permission of the publisher,
or in accordance with the provisions
of the Copyright Act 1956 (as amended).

Any person who commits any unauthorised act in relation to
this publication may be liable to criminal
prosecution and civil claims for damage.

A CIP catalogue record for this title is
available from the British Library.

ISBN: 978-1-80439-178-5

This is a work of fiction.
Names, characters, places and incidents originate from the writer's
imagination. Any resemblance to actual persons, living or dead, is
purely coincidental.

First Published in 2024

Olympia Publishers
Tallis House
2 Tallis Street
London
EC4Y 0AB

Printed in Great Britain

Dedication

I dedicate this work to everyone who has supported me throughout the process – family, friends and the editorial team. Thank you to you all. I also dedicate this book to all comfort women and all the victims of the war I have used as inspiration for this story. There are no winners in battles where lives are lost.

Rosei-ga yume-no
  cho-wa orisue

The butterflies in Rosei's dream
  would be origami

– Ihara Saikaku

PROLOGUE

The best way to defeat an enemy is by seeing them as your worst personal fear. The fear you would die to overcome.

I prefer the open fields. The breeze of the landscapes shaking the trees calms me. The sunrise never disappoints to show its beauty.

The butterflies pass by, flying on top of my head, my fingers around my sword in a tight grasp. I know she's watching.

I close my eyes and take a deep breath, meditating. I let the sounds of the birds take me far away. This battle can be my last. But I am ready.

It is time to fight.

PART I

悲しみ – kanashimi

(sorrow)

1

Ayana opened her eyes before the Sun could even rise. She woke up as if she hasn't fallen asleep at all.

Getting out of bed, she went straight to the bath house. Without worrying if anyone would wake, Ayana went down the wooden stairs in a rush, crossing the small back yard. It was a cold, cloudy morning. The raindrops made a faint noise when falling on to the wooden floor. There was a gloomy aspect to that morning, a sleepy cold forming smokes out of breath.

For contrast, Ayana threw herself in the hottest water, feeling chills down her spine, waking up. Feeling the warmth wash her body, face and mouth, Ayana calmed down. She took deep breaths, letting the water do its course from the top of her head to her toes. She tried to find as much comfort as she could from the water.

"Everything is going to be all right," she whispered, for the millionth time, while drying herself in a rush and dressing up again in the creamy-coloured robe she came in. Outside, she was, once again, cold.

She put on her shoes and rushed back to the main building, her hair soaking in all the rain water. She crossed the big saloon with its massive flower jars, its paintings and its round wooden table in the middle, where a maid was cleaning, then passing through the narrow hallways, seeing the waking silhouettes of the other girls through the bamboo doors.

Back to her room, a modest square with not much but a

messy bed and a wall-size closet full of kimonos, Ayana sat in front of her mirror and makeups. Brushing her rain-wet hair, she contemplated her early-bird appearance. She didn't think of herself as unpleasant – she was a little tall for someone her age, had fair skin that bared thin brows, deep eyes, a straight nose, thin lips and a strong jaw. She needed those features to be always delicate, even though they still failed and showed her resilience. Her hairs ran long and straight down her chest, wet. She was way too used to seeing herself.

But she attracted many men to the okiya, which pleased Koyuki-san very much.

And today was the day she would proceed with the results of her mizuage. The bidding over her was a difficult dispute – the okiya already had a record of ten thousand yen collected by Shizu. And now twenty thousand, from Ayana. A lot of teahouses were talking about Koyuki-san's new breaking record. About the most famous geisha at the moment in Kyoto – Hanako. She was a hard-working maiko and people noticed it. That eagerness of hers was enough to make her rise as a geisha eventually, having a debut that was already expected from the public. Since her recent collar change, she started feeling the pressure of her responsibilities with the Hirata house more than ever.

Diverging her attention from her reflection to a picture up on her mirror, Ayana extended her arm to reach it. It was a photograph of herself as a baby, with her mother and grandmother. They were both geishas and would be so proud of her if they were there right now. Ayana brushed her fingertips against the dusty photograph, a melancholic smile on her face. She turned into the Hanako they had expected her to be.

A knock at the door startled the girl.

"Come in!" she called, putting the photograph back in its

place.

The door slowly sled open. It was Koyuki-san. She walked up to Ayana, her dark robe static amid the light movement of her knees, as if she were floating. That was how they learned to walk.

"You don't have to put on your makeup now," said the woman, sitting next to the girl. Her dark hair was tied in a delicate bun, some grey shining on the black. Ayana could see the hard work around the woman's eyes. "Rest for tonight until you have to get your hair done and the dresser comes to get you ready."

Ayana took a deep breath. She was physically tired, but her mind was racing.

"I'm just nervous. I want to do a good job."

Koyuki-san laughed, her complexion becoming younger for a second. The woman picked the brush and caressed Ayana's hair, calming the girl down. The soft fur was therapeutic against Ayana's scalp. She closed her eyes.

"You have nothing to do that you have never done before. Just be quiet, smile, serve and look pretty. And try not to exhaust yourself with pessimistic thoughts. One of the girls will bring your breakfast."

Koyuki-san started to organize the messy room while complaining about it, although Ayana did not pay much attention, dozing off at some point. She opened her eyes again with Koyuki-san holding her elbow and instructing her to go to bed. With a blurry vision, Ayana saw the door closing.

She was to go to a nearby teahouse and entertain some men with Koyuki-san later at night. One in particular grew fond of her – Imamura-senpai. He was a young man in the army. That was not going to be their first time meeting or talking, and Ayana knew he was going to analyse her like a soldier studies their enemy. He always had a cold, judgemental gaze within him that went well with his stiff posture.

The first time she saw him was eight months prior. Koyuki-san was training her and Rikiya as young maikos. She was there to meet some friends and the gentleman that had his eyes on Shizu. He had a proposal to make and she already imagined what it could be.

"I overheard their conversation one day," Rikiya whispered to Ayana, amid the distraction of others. She glanced over to the middle aged man drinking his sake at the other side of the table. "He wants to keep Shizu as a wife for his son, but Koyuki-san doesn't want him to, of course."

Ayana's eyes opened wide.

"Really?"

Rikiya nodded, her eyes lighter than usual against the lamplight. Her ornaments giggled along with her head and some of her dark hair fell on her face. Ayana put them behind the girl's ears. Rikiya was a petite girl, and her thick hair made up for the weight she didn't have.

Their conversation was interrupted by one of the men asking Rikiya a question about some subject they were talking about before. Ayana was too immersed in her thoughts to pay attention to what it was. Now she understood why Shizu didn't come with them – Koyuki-san wanted to make sure that old man didn't see her geisha, and just forgot about her eventually. She knew how to open opportunities for her girls, but she also knew how to be protective of them.

That was when their eyes locked.

Ayana distractedly looked up to a man who was already staring at her. He was young. He was smiling.

"Could you pour me some sake, please?" he asked, as if he had rehearsed that line in his mind a hundred times before. Ayana liked how he was so polite to her, speaking softly amid all the loud laughs around them. It was all a contrast to his harsh eyes. She avoided looking at them. They were like blades.

She crawled a little towards his corner and poured him the drink until his cup was full, making sure to quickly look at him once, as Koyuki-san had taught.

"Thank you," he said, sipping on his drink, eyes still on her. Ayana pretended to be busy and did not say anything.

She poured him sake once more later on, besides showing to be engaged in the conversations they were all having. She noticed him gaze at her constantly, which gave her chills down her spine.

They met again two months later, at a party, shortly after Ayana's debut as a geisha. She was alone with Koyuki-san this time.

Word came to the woman that he had his eyes on Ayana. For her desperation, Koyuki-san loved that. She was eager to set future meetings between them.

Later that night, when Koyuki-san got too distracted to watch over Ayana, the girl started strolling around the grounds, occasionally stopping to greet people and take pictures. That was when she felt a pat on her shoulder.

It was the soldier. His beard had grown.

"We meet again," he said. His voice was still the same – a forced roughness to it.

She bowed.

"Hello… uh..."

He laughed, his eyes switching to a childish look for one split second.

"Imamura-senpai," he said, being serious again. "I thought you would remember that."

Ayana shily smiled and started to walk away from him.

"I am sorry."

"Wait!," he called. Ayana startled.

He walked and stopped in front of her.

"Pardon me, I forget a lot of things myself," he said, his voice soft again. "You can call me Taichi."

Ayana bowed once again.

"My name is Hanako."

"My pleasure," he said, smiling once again, revealing a bright set of teeth. "Would you like to take a walk?"

Ayana nodded and so, they started walking.

Taichi, all that time, was talking about his life. He mentioned his childhood with his housewife mother and army father. He grew up with a strict parent he lost for the war. The army was all he knew. Ayana got a bit tired, but was glad that, so far, he hadn't asked any questions about her. Her life was not interesting. In her opinion, his life was not interesting either – but no one really wanted to hear what mysteries geishas had with them.

They arrived at a small bridge, where people would occasionally walk past the lake under it. Ayana walked closer to the edge, taking a look at the water. There were pink flowers floating atop orange fishes. Despite being dark, the moonlight made small white dots shine whenever the fresh wind blew little waves in the lake.

"So…" Taichi whispered. He was very close to Ayana, his arms hanging from the bridge as he was leaning against it. Ayana imagined what was going to come next. "How come are we both here, talking, right now?"

Ayana discreetly took a deep breath. *You were the only one talking*, she thought to herself.

"You want to know how I became a geisha?"

Taichi nodded. Ayana shily smiled.

"My grandmother was a geisha. I don't remember her because she passed away when I was a baby. My mum was the one telling me everything about her and teaching me all she learned because she was also a geisha. My mother is the daughter of a business man who showed interest in my grandmother. And my father was a tenant. He even proposed to my mother and she refused, but still had me. I never met him or my grandfather."

Taichi's eyebrows lifted when she mentioned her father. He insisted on trying to get more details out of her – perhaps he knew the man – but got nothing. Seeing his frustration, Ayana apologized and turned to leave. He hurried his steps to reach her, saying there was nothing to apologize for. They walked back in eerie silence.

A light knock woke Ayana up. The door sled and there was Mameko, holding a tray.

"Hello, Hanako-senpai," Mameko sang. Ayana smiled back while the girl closed the door and walked towards her, putting the tray down, her bangs waving along with the movement of her steps.

Ayana looked down to see a rice bowl, three onigiris and ten slices of sashimi, with ginger on the side. There was also a cup and a teapot.

"This is a very colourful tray," she said, looking at Mameko. "Thank you."

The maiko sat down. Her big, innocent eyes stared back at Ayana.

"Koyuki-san wants you to rehearse some things," she said. "Like your dance and serving tea. So I can help you."

Ayana nodded, excited with the idea of tutoring her friend. She started serving tea and explaining it step by step. Once she was done eating, she rehearsed her dance for the night, while Mameko played the shamisen.

The girls were interrupted by the sound of the door sliding once again. It was Shizu. She was almost as tall as the doorway.

Ayana's eyes shined. Shizu had had a troubled childhood. At the age of six, she ran away from home, knocked at Koyuki-san's door by chance and begged to come in for the night because she was hungry and wanted somewhere warm to sleep in. She ended up staying for good. Her parents never objected – they knew Koyuki-san would provide her with things they never could.

She was already a maiko when Ayana came into the okiya. For a long time, Shizu was the only geisha there that had her mizuage so high – that is, until Ayana's. Even then, Shizu was the chosen one by Koyuki-san to be the atotori, and rule the okiya when the time came. She was indeed destined to be a great geisha, and Ayana respected her a lot for that.

Mameko got up to leave because she figured she should let the other two alone. When she was about to get past the door, Shizu grabbed her hand.

"Stay," she said, taking a deep breath. She seemed nervous. "I told Rikiya to come here soon. We need to talk before taking our conversation to Koyuki-san."

Mameko and Ayana exchanged confused looks.

Shizu took a letter out of her robe. At that very moment, Rikiya entered the room.

"Are we all showing Hanako-senpai support today?" she sang, passing through the door without looking at the other two and sitting on the floor, her red silk robe shining. Seeing that the other girls were serious, she raised her thick eyebrows. "Girls… why aren't you excited?"

Shizu didn't take her narrowed eyes off what was on her

hands.

"I really need all of you to read this letter," she said. "It's from Hina."

Ayana was not understanding.

In fact, none of them were. Ayana could feel a heavy air in the room. If she extended her arm up, she could touch it.

Shizu opened the letter and read it out loud:

"Dear friends…," she started. "It's me, Hina. Since I came back, I have been trying to write to you. I am currently away from home and from my family, somewhere strange with many other women. They won't tell us anything."

Shizu's voice cracked, and she looked around in frustration. The girls were now focused on the message, while the air closed down on them. Ayana found it hard to breathe.

Shizu went on:

"People are talking about a war, and I probably risked some lives to deliver this message to you. Something bad is about to happen. So please, be safe. Love you all."

Shizu put the note down. Ayana's heart was beating as fast as ever, and she feared she could be heard by the others.

Hina came to Japan because her father was doing labour work. She adopted a Japanese name and learned the language during her years living in Kyoto. She met Ayana at a market. The girls became very good friends and Hina constantly showed up at the okiya.

One night, she gave them the news she had to leave soon. The girls thought this would be good for her – to finally go back home. They wrote several letters to her ever since, always waiting for a response.

Now, the wait was over.

"We need to know if Hina is safe," Shizu said, her thin brows curving in sorrow. "But I just don't know how. There's no other information in here."

"Who gave you this letter?" Mameko asked.

"I don't know," Shizu replied with a sigh. "One of the maids just found it outside along with the other letters."

Ayana shook her head. All they knew was that Hina was in danger, hiding from someone, somewhere unknown. And they needed to find her no matter what.

That night, Ayana wore a dark pink kimono, with golden geometrical patterns and a light yellow obi – bright colours for a bright occasion, Koyuki-san said. She had her hair bun done since the morning, with golden ornaments, and her makeup recently applied – the white paste was still cold against her cheeks, but she still felt hot from the news she received in the morning. Koyuki-san was still unaware of the letter.

"You look beautiful," said the woman while they were walking to the teahouse. Ayana forced a smiled and thanked her.

The rain had long stopped and was exchanged for a warm air that perpetuated until late in the evening. The streets were dry and the nightlife was a contrast to the silent morning they had.

When they got to the entrance, Koyuki-san stopped. She turned around to face Ayana, very serious. Her worried expression did not match her vivid robes.

"Ayana-chan, my dear…," she started. She was the only one to call the girl by her real name when other people were not around. "I will be at that teahouse nearby," she said, pointing to an establishment a few steps away from them. "I was informed of a change of plans, but I couldn't disturb you."

"So… what is happening?" Ayana asked, apprehensive. The woman gave a faint smile, looking at Ayana with tenderness.

"You are to stay here with Imamura-senpai," she said. "I will come back as soon as I am done."

Koyuki-san hugged her and left, disappearing in the darkness of the street only to appear again under the light outside of the teahouse. She sled the door and got in, laughs emerging and falling silent once the door was closed. Sometimes, even Koyuki-san had to give in to some influences preyed upon her girls, and they could do nothing but understand.

So Ayana turned her attention back to the door in front of her, where Taichi was waiting right on the other side. She took a deep breath and opened the door with determination.

She just wanted to end this as fast as she could.

2

Ayana sled the door open only to see Taichi wearing nothing but a plain dark robe, sitting in front of a table for two. There were two cups and a teapot in front of him. His gaze was cold and fixed in Ayana, like he wanted to petrify her. She felt the hairs on her arms rise up.

"Hello, Hanako," he said, his voice deep like a well. He extended his hand in the direction of the table. "Please, sit."

Right away, Ayana walked in and sat, without taking her eyes off him.

There was a brief moment of silence. He kept looking at her.

"I was expecting to see other people here," she finally managed to say. Then, in an attempt to impress him and break the ice, she smiled. "But I think I actually prefer it this way."

Taichi blinked, surprised by her unexpected response.

"I thought we could get to know each other better alone," he explained. He started to smile. A quite sweet smile.

Ayana adjusted herself, leaning closer to him. She glanced at the cups and then back at him.

"Do you really think we need to waste time with tea? Shouldn't we drink something stronger?"

Taichi laughed and looked down, nervous. Whatever Ayana was doing seemed to be working.

"You're right," he answered, getting up quickly. "I will be right back."

He left through the door behind him and, as soon as he did,

Ayana started walking around the room, anxious. She needed a moment alone. To ground herself, she stared at the creamy walls with tree drawings, following the black twigs with the touch of her fingertips. In a slow pace, she looked around at the bamboo doors, the wooden table, the flat brown carpets. Trying to get a sense of the place.

She didn't know what to do or how to behave anymore. If he got mad, things would go wrong and it would be very bad for her and for the okiya. She had to make him pleased with her company, but she didn't want to stay.

By repeatedly whispering to herself to calm down, Ayana kept thinking about Koyuki-san's instructions – be as quiet as possible, cooperate with any wish, never show discomfort, be alert and awake.

The door sled open again and she stopped, standing in a corner, pretending to just look around, bored. She had her coloured fan out.

"Are you okay?" Taichi asked. He started to pour the drinks.

Ayana looked at him and smiled, trying to be spontaneous.

"Yes, I just find it a little hot in here," she said and walked slowly in his direction, in a snake-like way, without taking her eyes off him. Sitting again, she grabbed her cup and swallowed the drink in one go. "Should we play a game?" she asked, doing her best to hide her disgusted face. She never liked alcohol.

Taichi giggled and sat on his side of the table.

"All right, we can play," he said and poured her more drinks.

"Let's tell things about each other and having to guess what is true and what is not," she said. "If I say something true or false and you get it wrong, you drink. If you guess it correctly, I drink."

She leaned over to get her drink before he even said anything.

"I'll start," she said. He would occasionally giggle. "I have friends outside of my okiya. True or false?"

Taichi murmured, thinking. It seemed like a stupid question to him.

"I don't know... true?"

He was right. But she would never admit it.

"False," she sang, laughing.

"W-wait..." he murmured. "You are always going to social events and talking to people. Aren't you friends with them? What about me?"

Ayana started laughing. *Never would you be my friend*, she thought.

"Taichi, honey..." she started. "That's what we geishas are supposed to do. We can't leave the okiya much. Now drink."

He shrugged and drank. Then poured more. She wanted him to get drunk. Maybe he would eventually fall asleep.

"Okay, I don't like to lose," he said. He sat straight and squeezed his eyes while looking at her, studying her face again. "I was married before. True or false?"

Ayana remembered a story he told about breaking off an arranged engagement set up for him, saying it was because of his enlistment. But there was actually something about the woman that he didn't like – she was too much, he had said.

She narrowed her eyes back at him. If she felt bothered by it, he had to feel bothered as well.

"You were... almost married."

Taichi was actually surprised.

"So you remember. Good!" he said, and drank. He gasped and looked at his drink. "This is a little strong. And I see you are already a little off yourself."

Ayana laughed. She was not going to let him get away easy.

"How about... you guess things about me instead, then?"

Taichi blinked, confused.

"But... how am I going to come up with facts about you if I don't know you well?"

She started laughing again.

"Oh, Taichi," she said, going to sit next to him. She stumbled on the way, to her surprise and disappointment. "You said yourself you wanted to get to know me better, so let's have fun with it."

She touched his shoulder. He shrugged.

"Hanako is a fake name."

Ayana laughed.

"That is... correct."

She could have lied, but she was too dizzy to think strategically.

"What is your real name?" he asked her, getting closer.

Ayana opened her mouth to reply, trying to show she was not intimidated by him, but failed. His bladelike eyes were sharp looking at hers, making her hold her breath with tension.

"I... can't tell you," she answered, lowering her gaze. She drank more.

Perhaps it wouldn't be easy getting him drunk, she thought. She, however, was already halfway there. She could feel her cheeks burning.

"Sorry..." she whispered. "Alcohol slows me down," she laughed, trying to change the subject back to the game. "But... I think... you are an only child," she pointed at him, smiling like she was his comrade. "Am I right?"

Taichi laughed softly while extending a cup to her.

"I told you I have a younger brother..." he looked at her and signalled to the cup. "Now drink and tell me your name."

Ayana drank. When she turned her head back down, things

started to change around her. Even Taichi's gaze wasn't looking that cold anymore. He was acting kinder and – the worst – she never thought he was bad looking. Now she was sure he wasn't bad looking at all.

Ayana grunted after putting her cup down.

"I… feel… weird," she whispered, feeling her breath cold and salty.

"I think you had enough for today," Taichi said, getting up and then getting her up by her elbows.

"No," she protested, trying to put strength on her legs to stay sit. "I am okay."

"No, you're not," he chuckled, succeeding in getting her up on her feet. "Let's go."

He led her to another door. Ayana noticed they were in a teahouse, but not in a common area anymore. When Taichi left to get the sake, he had gone through a door which probably led to where other people were staying. The door he was leading her to right now, however, was a different one. An improvised bedroom.

It was small. It had nothing but a mattress and a lamp on the side. Ayana thought it looked warm, and she was suddenly feeling very tired. If only the situation was different, she mourned, she would enjoy laying there with a hot cup of tea and a book.

"Sit down," Taichi commanded. She did, for the lack of choice, and he crouched in front of her. He started to undo her hair bun and remove her ornaments. "Close your eyes and take deep breaths."

Ayana obeyed him. She did not want to, but there was nothing she else could do.

She felt her hair fall to her back, softly. Taichi massaged her scalp slowly, his fingertips barely being felt by her while making circular movements on her head. He also had a moist, warm cloth he gently rubbed against her face, followed by a dry cloth. He then held her cheeks.

"What is your name?" he whispered, his face very close to hers. "Who are you?"

Ayana remained quiet, her eyes still closed. She felt his warm breath closer and closer. Then, she felt his lips. They were gentle.

Her heart was beating so fast, she was having difficulty in breathing, but Taichi mistook it for excitement, as he was making the same sounds. Soon, she felt herself leaning backwards against her will, and he was on top of her, undoing her robe. She squeezed her eyes even more shut, while he moved his mouth to her neck. She tried to focus on her breath only and nothing else.

She only went to open her eyes again when Taichi's weight moved to her side. She turned around immediately, facing the yellow wall. She had the feeling his eyes were on her, which made her feel ashamed. He had seen the front of her naked body and now was seeing the back of it, when she actually did not want him to have seen anything at all.

She felt him move and the light was off. He moved again and she felt a blanket covering her. For a brief second, she was thankful, until she also felt Taichi's arm around her. They were both under the blanket.

"Good job," he whispered. Wondering when Koyuki-san would show up, Ayana closed her teary eyes, thanking the room for being dark.

A pale light woke her up, but she felt like she hadn't slept at all. She looked at herself and noticed she was in the same position from the night before, the blanket still on her. She turned her head and saw that Taichi was not next to her. Instead, he was sitting at the edge of the mattress, smoking.

She sat down. Her head was hurting.

He looked at her, seeing that she had the blanket covering most of her body except for her left shoulder and a bit of cleavage. Her hair fell gracefully on her face.

"You look beautiful," he said, turning his head away, as if he did not want to be distracted by her. "Too bad I have to leave soon."

"Where are you going?" she asked, although she couldn't care less.

He turned to face her again, his shoulder gently touching hers.

"Manchuria."

Ayana's eyes were wide. She gasped and covered her mouth. She couldn't believe what was going on.

For Taichi to be in the army and be going abroad, he could know what Hina talked about in her letter. He would know about the war and anything related to it.

Ayana opened her mouth to ask, but something stopped her – a feeling. Perhaps she shouldn't be so direct.

Taichi had a confused look on his face.

Ayana laughed, awkwardly.

"I'm sorry…" she managed to say. "This just sounds… nice. I never left here."

Taichi shrugged.

"Well, it is not very far," he said. "It became part of our empire not long before you were born, and we go there and back since then."

Ayana needed more. She could not let him go. Not now that things were starting to make sense.

"What do you do there?"

He looked around, uncomfortable.

"We keep an eye on things, but mainly follow orders. Not much that I can tell you," he answered, without looking at her.

"Well…" Ayana started, as if this all sounded very exciting for her. As if she thought Taichi was an important figure. She leaned her chin on his shoulder. "When are you going to be back?"

He looked at her and chuckled, like she was a funny little girl. He pinched her chin.

"In a couple of weeks," he said. "And we will meet again once I do, don't worry."

He seemed almost ready to leave. Ayana had to slow him down and dress up fast if she wanted to get more information from him. She got up and, on purpose, let the blanket fall like a curtain. Taichi looked at her up and down several times while she got dressed. She acted as if she hadn't noticed.

She remembered every word written in Hina's letter. If a war were to happen and they were one empire, the army needed to have something to do with whatever was going on with her friend. Or, at least, have the knowledge of any chaos.

"While you don't…" she started. "I mean… are there other women there? Do they have geishas?"

Ayana figured she could be a bit direct indeed. Such a question did not sound unusual given who she was and what she did for a living. There was no way he could suspect.

"Well, I guess," he said, not seeming to think much of it. "Every place has its own entertainments."

Ayana bit her lip upon hearing how he thought so wrong of her. But there it was – the clue she was looking for.

He sled the door open, entering the room where they were drinking at the previous night. Ayana followed him. They went out to the street. It was cold and quiet, barely anyone outside.

This time, there was no rain.

Taichi turned to face Ayana. He looked as if he had slept soundly. His face was jovial, though his eyes were still cold.

"I enjoyed last night," he looked her in the eyes. "I will be back before you even know it."

Having said that, he bowed to Ayana and left, just like that.

When he was out of sight, she ran back to the okiya, ignoring the looks the merchants were giving her. She banged on the door angrily and loud, calling for someone. When it opened, Ayana saw Koyuki-san and grabbed her arm.

"We need to talk with the girls!"

"Ayana-chan!" the woman called, holding both her shoulders. "Where were you? I went to get you, but they told me you had left. But you weren't here either. I was so worried!"

Koyuki-san had anxious eyes and purple bags under them. She hasn't got any sleep.

"I…" Ayana started, suddenly not knowing what to say. "We were there," she whispered.

She felt her eyes get teary, blurring her vision although no tears dared to fall. The remembrance of the previous night made the girl recall how uncomfortable, powerless and vulnerable she felt.

The woman hugged her tight, muttering apologies.

"Let's go inside for you to have the care you need," she said, looking at Ayana with pitiful eyes and guiding her to the okiya.

But Ayana grabbed her arm, alarmed again.

"I need to talk to the girls and it's important."

Before the woman could asked any further questions, Ayana heard steps and looked in their direction. It was Shizu, followed by the others. They were looking anxious. The stayed in silence for a long time, waiting for Ayana to say something.

"What is happening?" Koyuki-san demanded. She was sure there was something else going on.

Shizu stepped forward.

"There's something we need to tell you," she answered. "It's about Hina."

3

Ayana looked around her. They were all sitting around a rectangular wooden table, Mameko on one of her sides and Rikiya by her left. The light was weak and the room was dark, even though it was just morning. Whenever Koyuki-san needed privacy, she would close all the windows and doors form her office. The place looked as if it was night and the moon shined only there, for them.

Only five minutes ago, they were all at the front yard. Koyuki-san then started to walk and called the geishas inside in a sharp way. She closed her entire office so as to not be disturbed. The girls then sat around the table in silence, waiting.

The truth was that Koyuki-san grew fond of Hina when they met. She was just a very young girl in a strange land – a land where she should never have been in the first place.

"Listen…" she started, after a minute of silence, organizing her thoughts. She folded her long fingers on the table. "I want to know what you know."

Shizu sled the letter on the table, as if she were ready to have this conversation. It impressed Ayana how Shizu could predict Koyuki-san's actions so easily.

Koyuki-san read it fast – there wasn't much on it. She spent more time processing the message instead.

She looked up to make sure all four of them were attentive.

"Do any of you know what Hina is talking about?"

They all shook their heads, except for Ayana.

"Imamura-senpai mentioned something about leaving for Manchuria."

Koyuki-san frowned.

"Could you elaborate on that?"

Ayana adjusted herself to sit more comfortably, and told them about her night.

"I just connected the points," she said. "Hina said a war is coming… I just thought the army would have something to do with this."

There was a long, tense silence. Again, Ayana felt as if the air was heavy and she could reach for it.

"What do we do now?" Mameko voiced the doubt they all had pairing over their heads.

"We have to go find her," Rikiya said.

They all looked at her. She shrugged.

"What? If we want to know where our friend is, we have to look for her, even though she didn't ask for our help. Or we will remain with this doubt forever – if she is okay or not. And she probably isn't."

"I can't let you," voiced Koyuki-san. "Taking all of you at once is way too suspicious."

"Maybe not all of us go," said Shizu. She got up, a shine in her eyes. She looked at Ayana. "You go, Hanako-chan!"

Ayana opened her mouth, but didn't protest. It made sense. She was the only link between them and the army.

"Yes!" exclaimed Rikiya, touching Ayana's arm with excitement. She looked at Koyuki-san. "We should convince Imamura-senpai of taking Hanako-senpai with him to Manchuria!"

Koyuki-san looked at Ayana, her lips pressed. She valued the safety of her geishas too much.

"I don't think this is a good idea," she said. "But we will solve this," she added, before anyone could protest.

She gestured for the girls to leave while reaching for her phone. The girls knew no one was supposed to hear any calls from Koyuki-san.

Koyuki-san got up, now alone in the room. She knew Imamura-senpai was attending an event before his departure, and she had been invited even before arranging him with Ayana. She just didn't see any reason to confirm her presence just yet – until now. She called her friend, the host, to confirm she was going with her newest geisha.

"We will be delighted to have you," her friend said. Koyuki-san thanked him and hung up. In seconds, she had done things impulsively and that was not like her at all.

With her hands sustaining her head, she took several deep breaths until a tear dropped at her table, leading to a soft, silent cry. Whatever that girl was going through, she did not deserve it.

ƐЖЗ

Ayana left the okiya with a coin. She wanted to go to a temple and pray.

On the previous night, Koyuki-san informed her of a party to attend, and that Imamura-senpai would be there. Ayana hated the news, but there was nothing she could do besides hoping everything would turn out well.

The weather that morning was cloudy and cold. Ayana thought she felt the same. It was like the sky knew how her heart was feeling. Inside the temple, the sound of rain felt distant. The place was dry and calm, silent – a contrast to the outside. There were only a few people praying.

Ayana threw her coin and rang the bell. She wished for guidance and luck.

"Hey," she heard a soft voice say. She turned around.

"Kiyoshi-senpai," she whispered, surprised.

Kiyoshi Saito was a childhood friend. Since she started working at the okiya at a young age, Ayana used to arrange some time here and there to play with him, Shizu and the siblings Yasuo and Yoshiki.

She felt there was always a special connection between her and Kiyoshi and she knew he could feel the same. The same excitement upon seeing each other and the same longing to spend time together once again. But as time passed, they grew distant. Ayana missed him at first, but figured that was how life worked.

Kiyoshi looked her up and down. He gestured to the back of his head.

"I see you changed your hair style."

"Yes…" she answered. "I turned my collar."

"Oh, I heard," he said. "I… I guess I am happy for you?" He was shy, but saw Ayana had no reaction. "Are *you* happy?" he asked.

Ayana shrugged and took a deep breath.

"I guess I am," she replied. She could only tell him that much.

Kiyoshi looked down, with his hands on his pockets. His arms were stronger and tanner than she remembered.

"That's good," he whispered. "So, will you be busy?"

"Probably," she answered, wishing she could say otherwise. It was a strange conversation.

She tried to smile. To lift the mood or change the subject.

"How are the brothers?" she asked.

Kiyoshi also tried to smile, and it was a good effort.

"They are good," he replied. "We are doing the usual… you

know, selling fruits and vegetables, fixing bicycles... sometimes getting into trouble."

Ayana gave a genuine laugh.

Kiyoshi, Yasuo and Yoshiki always showed themselves to be energetic young boys. They liked to run, jump, and fight. Yasuo even knew how to use swords.

"I remember you three used to have a club," she said. "And no girls were allowed."

Kiyoshi laughed loud. His laugh echoed in the temple and mixed in with the sound of the bells.

"I wanted to open an exception for you, but they didn't let me! They thought you wouldn't be good with a sword."

Ayana opened her mouth in false shock, pretending to be offended.

"I bet I would be very good with swords," she said, her hand on her chest. "I am a brave girl."

"I know you are," he said, serious, in a low tone. He looked at the direction of his stand. "I have to go back. But tell me if you want me to teach you how to fight. The club doesn't exist anymore, so we should be good."

Ayana smiled and nodded.

"It was good to see you."

He left running, as usual. Ayana looked at him from a distance, being nostalgic for a few seconds. He was not a young boy anymore, but that energy she knew still remained vivid in him.

ƐЖ3

A couple of nights later, Ayana was once again getting dressed for Taichi. With a dark robe, she looked at herself in the mirror, analysing the star pattern the outfit had. It was a kimono like no other – all her layers were black, with the top one being a dark violet colour. The very bottom of the dress and sleeves shone in silver, spread around the fabric and were stronger at the edges. The obi around her was white like a pearl. Ayana had the moon and stars covering her body.

"You look like the night sky," Mameko whispered, eyes wide with admiration. She was right. Koyuki-san was always able to arrange such pieces, and the girls were always impressed. Ayana's hair was brushed back, with the two sides forming triangles and coming together in a tall bun, with silver ornaments to match the rest of the outfit. Ayana knew she was never wearing that kimono again.

During all the way to the party, Koyuki-san squeezed Ayana's hands and didn't let go. She had been quiet since the reunion with the girls, and stayed in her office with doors closed the entire time, only leaving for that specific night. Ayana knew she was far from agreeing with this plan, but there was nothing better to be done.

They arrived at the party, a celebration a businessman was throwing to some friends who had just arrived in town. Ayana and Koyuki-san entered the mansion, greeting people on the way. Koyuki-san was anxiously looking around.

"I need you to just find someone and get distracted with conversation," she told Ayana. "But don't stay out of sight."

With that, she let go of Ayana's hand and started wandering around the garden. Ayana didn't find it difficult to exchange words with someone every once in a while – she had never seen so many people gathered like that before. The hard part was to keep track of Koyuki-san in the crowded darkness. While saying hello and making small talk to guests, Ayana would excuse herself whenever she couldn't see the woman anymore, then walk around looking for her.

It took a while, however, for them to find Taichi. Ayana actually saw him before Koyuki-san did. She heard a voice yell his name and then some laughs. She was taking a picture with a woman that found her robe marvellous, when she saw him walking right past her. She quickly smiled to the guest and turned away as soon as the flash clicked.

Keeping a safe distance, she looked for both him and Koyuki-san. They were standing close to each other, but the woman couldn't tell who he was by only looking at his back. Ayana then kept her eyes fixed on Koyuki-san, waving her fan frenetically in the air. The woman, looking around, locked eyes with the girl. Ayana tilted her head in the direction of Taichi and Koyuki-san got close to him and the person he was talking to. Ayana turned around and stayed close enough to hear some of the conversation.

She heard when he asked how Koyuki-san was doing and the small talk she was making about his trip until mentioning what Ayana had told about their night.

"She commented how she was very nervous and feared she had done something wrong," Koyuki-san said in a pity tone. "Did everything turn out fine?"

"Oh yes, no worries," Taichi said, followed by something Ayana couldn't catch.

There was more small talk and then a tone of question. Koyuki-san was now probably using all her charm to convince him to spit something about Manchuria. Koyuki-san was very good at manipulating people when she wanted. She had good communication skills and was very smart.

The conversation seemed to keep dragging itself, and Ayana couldn't hear a thing. She started to get distracted with some men nearby who complimented her. She now just had to wait.

She gasped when she turned around and saw Taichi right behind her.

"Oh," she whispered, bowing. "Hello, Imamura-senpai."

He laughed.

"You look beautiful, Hanako-chan," he said.

"Thank you, Imamura-senpai," she said. He laughed again.

"Why so formal? Don't be shy; come take a walk with me."

He offered his arm and Ayana took it. They started walking to a quieter part of the garden.

"So…" he started, after a long silence. "Koyuki-san told me about a friend of yours that you really want to visit."

Ayana pretended to be surprised.

"Did she?"

Taichi nodded, serious.

"She asked if I could take you with me and I said I would see to it," he answered. "But I preferred to tell you the answer in person."

Ayana rushed to stand in front of him, startling him. She didn't mean it. She was just anxious with the possible answer.

"So you are taking me with you?" she asked, urgency in her eyes.

He sighed.

"There's a lot of confidential things wherever we are located," he answered. "Manchuria is a very rich land, and its conquest was possible thanks to the Emperor. It's not a place one can tourist around."

"I promise I won't disturb in any way," Ayana replied. "Let me see my friend, please." She bowed very low.

Taichi shook his head again, and simply kept walking.

"We can't allow it," he said. "There's no business a geisha

can do abroad."

Ayana forced to keep her voice steady.

"I would keep you company..."

They continued to walk in silence. The voices now were further away, there weren't so many lights in that area. Nothing except for a tree and a bench. The moon illuminated the space a little.

Without thinking much, Ayana sat in the bench, feeling that she had to process all the information. She felt stupid and naïve.

Taichi sat next to her. She flinched for a second. She forgot he was still there.

"I will be very busy and will stay there for a while," he said, his voice firm. "So you would be alone a lot."

Ayana blinked.

"What?" she whispered.

Taichi kept his eyes fixated on her.

"If it depended on me, you would come," he said. "But such a request is beyond my powers."

Ayana gulped. She fought back tears and hoped Taichi hadn't noticed them.

"I am sorry if Koyuki-san and I wasted your time," she whispered, not able to meet his gaze.

She stood up to leave, but he held her hand. She shivered.

"There's nothing wrong with asking," he said, and a smile crossed his face. "In fact, Koyuki-san almost convinced me. Taking you with me is very tempting."

Ayana forced a shy smile.

"Well..." Taichi said, also getting up. "I will get us both something to drink, so don't leave."

He fixed his suit and turned to look at her up and down.

"Did I already say you look stunning tonight?" he asked,

kissing her hand and leaving as if she weren't there and he hadn't said a word.

From that moment on, Ayana felt disgust towards his inconstancy and his games.

Back in her room, Ayana spent the remainder of her night pacing around. She had to go. She had to find a way to get through Taichi in the next day, somehow. If her connection with him was of no use, she needed other alternatives.

But first, she had to pack.

In a brown-leather case, she put some hair ornaments, her brushes, and some robes. She was opening boxes and drawers in search of something important she could be forgetting – anything.

Inside a small rectangular red box, Ayana found a photograph of a house with a lake on the side and a tree. For a brief second, it didn't look like any house she has ever seen in the street, but it wasn't unfamiliar either. Then, focusing on the image, she remembered – it was Hina's house. In the back of the photo, there was a message:

Ayana-senpai,
    I will miss the moments we shared together.
    Take this photograph as a souvenir. It's my home.
    So you can look at it and go visit me there one day!

In smaller calligraphy, there was an address, at the very bottom of the paper. Ayana remembered well the day she received this. Hina had given pictures with different messages to all the girls in the okiya. She cried when she gave Ayana hers, really hoping they could see each other again. Hina was a very emotional girl. Ayana promised she would stop by someday, and she really held on to that promise.

And now there was the day. How convenient, Ayana thought, to think that Hina would tell her friends where she lived and hope they would show up. It was almost as if she knew what the future was reserving for them.

But then again, maybe she did.

Ayana wished those were not the circumstances of her visit.

Putting the photograph inside her luggage, she concluded there was nothing more that mattered. She had with her everything that was important.

Curling herself to sleep, Ayana prayed to find answers and, mostly, find her friend.

4

It was a rainy morning when Ayana left the okiya once again. *Come and stay locked up with me*, Taichi had said, letting the alcohol take most of his shame away. *I promise I won't let anyone see you.*

She had succeeded to get him drunk at the party and convince him to take her along in his travel. She ran back to the okiya without Koyuki-san knowing, before leaving again so early the next day, glad that the woman was simply asleep in her bedroom. Ayana knew exactly where Taichi was, and did not want to waste any time – or be seen by anyone.

In a rickshaw, Ayana sat at the back, tapping her fingers around her leg anxiously. She jumped off as soon as the driver stopped, entering the teahouse Taichi was at – the same one they had spent a night together before.

Taichi was still asleep, so Ayana just dropped her suitcase and sat down, waiting. She did not take her eyes off him until he finally woke up. She didn't count how much time it took him to open his eyes and realise she was there.

He grunted and sat, looking at her for a long time with a confused expression in his eyes, until a sudden realization came through him.

"Oh," he whispered.

Ayana raised her eyebrows.

"So you remember," she stated.

Without looking at her, Taichi got up and got dressed. He

had a stern look on his face.

"I was drunk," he responded. "What I said doesn't change anything."

Ayana's heart started pounding fast and her palms got sweaty. She got up in a rush, ignoring the dizziness that came with it.

"You promised," she said, firmly.

He looked at her and shook his head. Nothing he said would make her leave.

"I was drunk," he repeated, as if to emphasize the excuse. "And you bewitched me."

Walking towards her, he held her chin up and looked her deep in her eyes, their noses touching. He stood as if he was going to kiss her, although their lips never touched. Ayana tried to calm her shivering.

"You really did," he whispered. Backing away from her, he turned around so as to not look at her, defeated. "When we get to the port, just stay close to me and keep a low profile. No one will ask questions."

For their entire ride to the port, Taichi did not look at her or touch her or talk to her. Ayana ended up falling asleep, only to wake up with the sound of a door closing. It was Taichi's door, and he was talking to the driver. They had arrived. She got out of the vehicle and waited for him. He got the bags and walked as if she weren't there. She went after him.

Some men stared, younger ones, but were too intimidated by Taichi to raise any eyebrows at him – the older men seemed to understand or, simply, not care about why she was there. Ayana just kept her gaze lowered to the ground until they arrived in a small room.

"You will stay here," Taichi said, dropping her things and

leaving her alone in the wooden-coloured square that would be her room for the next couple of days.

Time passed very slowly for Ayana. She didn't leave the room – where she was glad she could stay in, comfortably – and no one opened the door either. She thought Taichi made sure no men would bother her, but she was surprised *he* did not come to bother at all.

Until the day they actually arrived. Taichi opened the door and locked it behind him, sitting in a chair across from her. He seemed tired, with dark circles under his eyes. His clothes were now a badly pressed uniform.

"We are here," he whispered, without meeting her gaze. "Now, I don't know why you are so eager to stay… but whatever it is, don't complicate things for me," he looked up. "Don't stay out of my sight."

Ayana simply nodded. When he got up, she went outside right after him, ready to leave the ship.

On land, Ayana noticed how the place was a much simpler one from the streets she was used to seeing. Up until they got in another car, there wasn't much to see. What surprised her the most was the amount of Japanese people there – walking around, talking, and laughing. Like they really had taken control.

"Pay attention," said Taichi. Ayana looked at him. "We are taking you to your place, so look around to know where it is and don't get lost."

She turned her attention back to the empty streets. She didn't need or want Taichi telling her what to do. If she got lost, she could just be lost forever and never have to see him again.

The car stopped in a small group of houses. Taichi left the car and Ayana understood she was going to stay in one of those places.

"Here," he said, handing her keys. "This house was arranged for you to stay. There will be someone bringing you food and also cleaning. I will show up sometime later today or tomorrow, so just rest."

He wasn't looking at her in the eyes, so she just bowed and he left. She stayed there until the car disappeared, then turned to the house and didn't know what to do. She just wanted to look for her friend.

The door to the house opened and a woman bowed, gesturing for her to come in. Nervous, Ayana rushed inside.

The woman took her bag and walked away, Ayana following her. The house was fairly small and simple, not much different than her room at the okiya. There was a table with chairs and cupboards next to it, and a bed in a corner, close to the window. Ayana looked outside and realised that was just a part of the place. She probably wasn't allowed to go visit the rest.

The woman with her was young, but definitely older than her. Maybe in her thirties. She was petite and needed to take care of her teeth. Ayana imagined she had children and a husband. She and the woman didn't talk – just bowed. Communication was difficult.

She then left through the same door, leaving Ayana alone. She wasn't sure if she could leave or not. But she had to act fast if she wanted to find Hina. She couldn't waste time – the faster she went home, the better. Taichi wasn't even going to complain.

Ayana laid her small, brown suitcase on the floor and opened it. Inside a little pocket was the picture of Hina's house. She closed her bag and got up, about to leave, when the woman entered the room again. She had just gone somewhere to get food. Now she was holding a tray with a bowl of rice, meat on the side and a cup of tea.

Smiling, the woman kept saying something, a word. She repeated this word a few times. Ayana wasn't sure if she was telling her to eat or to sit.

"No, no, no," Ayana said, shaking her head. She gently pushed the tray in the woman's direction. "For you," she said and smiled. She knew the woman was not understanding her either.

The woman then put the tray down, confused. She asked a question, pointing at the food. Ayana didn't reply because she didn't know if the woman was making sure she wasn't going to eat or if she was asking if she herself could eat it.

Instead, Ayana showed her the picture. Hesitating, the woman held it and turned it to the other side, where the address was. She looked back at Ayana, who was now anxious.

"Where?" she asked. The woman noticed her discreet urgency. She realised the importance this had to the girl. Possibly the whole reason why she was there.

The woman then smiled and gestured for Ayana to follow her. Outside, she called someone. A boy showed up. "He should probably be ten years old, or a little less." Ayana looked at the small, skinny child with a pale face. "There was no way he was older than thirteen. If so, he needed better care."

The woman was probably his mother. She showed him the photograph and pointed at Ayana while speaking to him. He just agreed and gestured for Ayana to follow him. Ayana bowed to the woman and left with the boy.

She walked for a while, maybe twenty minutes. But this while went fast – she was too focused on her mission to keep track of anything, but she looked around little. And this little she saw surprised her – here and there she caught glimpses of Japanese soldiers. Of posters on the walls or pamphlets on the ground, with Japanese letters, telling people how great it is to be a part of Japan, or how they should unite to fight. Indeed a war was happening, Ayana thought. She was scared.

The boy then stopped walking and looked at Ayana. She rushed her step and got close to him, looking at the direction he was. In front of them, there was a small house with a little garden at the front, next to a tree. On the other side, a lake and a bridge that led to another house. She looked at the photograph and confirmed – it was Hina's home.

Ayana rushed inside, tripping twice before getting to the door. She stopped herself to breathe. It's not like Hina would be there. She looked around and saw that the garden actually looked unkept – it needed maintenance. The flowers were dead and wrinkled. The grass was torn. That meant there was nobody home. Ayana opened the door and got in.

The house was a mess. The bed had been thrown against the wall, there were papers everywhere on the floor, along with glass. There were blood stains too, up to the ceiling. A mirror was smashed. There were clothes everywhere. Ayana couldn't figure what had happened there.

A cracking sound made her startle and gasp. A man showed up. He seemed to be in his late forties and had a grey beard. He had dirty, simple clothes and was holding a broom.

"S-sorry…" she whispered and turned to leave.

"Hey," he said. She stopped and looked at him. "Japanese?" he asked. She nodded.

"What happened here?" she asked, after a moment of hesitation.

The man looked around and took a deep breath.

"Parents had no money and sold her to Japanese," the man said. "But parents resist because they were forced."

"Forced?"

The man gestured, rubbing his fingers.

"Money," he said. "Parents don't want her to be taken. So Japanese came to take her. And they give the soldier money. They die."

Ayana blinked. Her throat was dry and she wasn't sure she understood him.

"They're... dead?"

"Yes," he answered, as if it was obvious. "Parents die, Japanese take her. She disappear."

Ayana's eyes got full of water. Her vision blurred. There was no air inside the living room.

"And... Hina?"

The man shrugged.

"Japanese take her, she come back week later. Then they find her and kill parents and take her again."

Ayana put her hands on her face, thinking.

"So... she was found twice?"

The man simply nodded. He was direct, but there was a certain sadness in his eyes.

"I am neighbour, I saw," he said. "My niece was taken too."

"Where are they?" Ayana asked. Tears were now falling.

The man again shook his head, his voice cracking.

"We don't know. They come and they take."

Ayana couldn't believe it. The man gently put his hand on her shoulder. She put her hand on top of his.

"T-thank... you," she managed to whisper and left the house. It felt like leaving a box, like Ayana was fighting for her lungs in the brief moment she stayed there. A flush of air hit her as soon as she got to the doorway.

Outside, the little boy was still there, looking at the house, waiting for her. Ayana just walked past him, and he ran to be in front of her. Looking at her, he held her hand. She stopped, surprised. With a sad smile, the little boy just led her back to her place, holding her hand the entire time. Suddenly, it was as if she were the little child.

When they arrived, she curled herself in the bed and started crying while holding the photograph of her friend's house, now destroyed. She heard a young voice that she figured could only belong to the little boy. He was probably telling his mother what happened. The woman walked in, left a cup next to Ayana, then covered her with a blanket and looked at her for a moment, before walking away and closing the door, leaving Ayana in the dark.

But Ayana couldn't cry for long. She was interrupted when she felt something in her legs. It was a liquid, flushing out of her, gently. When Ayana got up, she saw blood had stained a part of the bed, part of her dress and had covered her legs. Ayana frowned. Her period wasn't supposed to start until the next month and even then, she never bled so much.

That's when it hit her.

With her eyes wide open, Ayana covered her mouth and fell on her knees, her crying becoming louder by the second. She choked, throwing up while trying to find air to breath. Again it was as if she was inside a box. There was no air. She could feel a soft rope closing on her neck.

The door to the room opened and Ayana heard the woman gasp and yell something – either a question or a command. Then the woman held her head, lifting her face, and spoke to Ayana in a very soft voice. She got up, lifting Ayana with her and taking her outside.

The woman led Ayana through another door, taking her to a bathroom. The woman then sat her in a chair and started preparing the water. She undressed Ayana, guided her inside the bathtub and washed her. She cleaned away the vomit and the blood from her body. Then she left Ayana there, alone. But Ayana didn't care. She didn't care about anything anymore.

After several minutes, the woman returned with clean clothes. She got Ayana out of the tub and dried her, putting her new clothes on. The woman took her back inside her room. Ayana sat on the now clean bed and was ready to lay down again when the woman started brushing her hair and singing a lullaby. She did this for a while and Ayana felt better. She wished she could just stay there, without Taichi. Just with the little boy and that angel of a woman taking care of her.

When the woman was done with her hair, she started massaging Ayana's shoulders and then moved to her hands, sitting in front of her. She started talking. Ayana had no idea what she was saying but, by her tone of voice, it seemed to be a casual conversation. Maybe she was telling her something about her childhood, or something the boy did when he was younger.

The woman then got up saying something while touching Ayana's shoulder. It was a sad tone. She left the room, closing the door. Ayana laid on the bed and slept quicker than she thought.

A knock on the door woke her up. It was Taichi. Behind him, the sky was dark.

"I see you have been treated like a queen," he said, walking in her direction. "How about you treat me like a king now?"

While saying this, he reached for her face but she turned it away and got up to stand away from him, the bed between them.

"Wow," he exclaimed, laughing. "You want to play hard to get?"

"Leave me alone," Ayana whispered.

Taichi laughed again.

"What's the matter?" he asked, as if he couldn't believe a

person like Ayana had problems or feelings.

She looked him dead in the eye. He didn't have to know about Hina – but he still needed to understand how he had made her feel miserable and used.

"I just found out I was pregnant."

There was a long silence. Taichi's eyes were wide open.

"W-what?" Taichi asked, without blinking. "Was?"

Ayana nodded firmly, looking at right at him. He was pale.

"I just lost it."

Taichi sat on a chair, not believing what she had just told him.

"Are you saying…" he started. "I was going to be a father?"

Ayana looked away and didn't respond. She couldn't believe how much he only cared about himself.

"I want to leave," she whispered. "I can't stay in this place any longer."

She heard him walking in her direction.

"You can't go now, you have to wait," he said in a soft voice, standing in front of her.

Ayana eventually looked at him once again, but angry. He made her so angry.

She slapped his face and started impatiently pacing around. Taichi just remained there, looking at nowhere, with a hand print on his cheek.

"I am just *tired* of having you telling me what to do!" she yelled. "I don't want to stay here anymore, I *can't*!"

Taichi walked in her direction once again and hugged her. She tried to back away and started punching his chest and back, but he didn't let go of her until she softened.

"I'm sorry," he whispered, taking his arms off her.

He then opened the door and left.

5

For three days, Ayana refused to leave the room. She wouldn't drink, nor eat, and slept for long periods of time. The woman, her caretaker, always tried to cheer her up – she was always bringing new meals, preparing the bath, taking the covers out for Ayana, opening the window. But the girl refused to move.

She found herself in a dark place, where she felt a constant chill. If she extended her hand to the front of her face, she would not be able to see it. The limbo took over her, embracing her in a tight gap.

Taichi was showing up every night. He would sit on a chair and stay still there for hours, trying to convince Ayana to eat properly.

"Please, Hanako," he would whisper. He was much calmer when speaking to her, like a total different person. "This depression is consuming you."

"Then let it do its job," she would snap.

He would then leave and show up the next day. The cycle would repeat itself.

On the third day, the maid entered the room and shook Ayana's shoulder. Ayana knew it was her because of the sound of her light, speedy steps. But something was different this time. She looked over and saw the man she had spoken to at Hina's house, behind the maid.

Ayana sat down for the first time in many hours. She felt dizzy right away. Her head hurt.

"I give this," he said, extending a photograph. Ayana took it. It was a happy Hina wearing a traditional dress, standing next to a girl dressed the same way as her. "Niece," the man said.

Ayana passed her fingers on the photograph. She had a weird feeling on her chest.

While she contemplated the picture, the woman spoke something to the man. It sounded like a question.

"Uh… miss," the man whispered. Ayana looked at him. He looked at the woman again and then back at Ayana. "Japanese man good?" he asked. He seemed a little uncomfortable, but suddenly eager to also know the answer.

That was what the woman wanted to know. She saw how Taichi treated her on their first day and heard all the fuss Ayana made. She didn't trust the army and was worried for Ayana's safety.

However, Ayana reflected on the answer. No, she did not consider him to be good to her. But, recently, he *seemed* to be caring. At the same time, it was obvious he was controlling her. And the woman knew what was his initial intention was in coming by every night.

But Ayana simply said he was good. She didn't want them to worry more than they were already.

She thanked the man for the picture, but it seemed they were not done. The woman kept talking to him and seemed to sound louder every time she said something. Ayana realised she was about to cry.

The man once again turned to her.

"Miss, we…" he started. "Want you safe. You good Japanese, don't stay with man," the woman pleaded something more and the man translated. "Stay."

Ayana shook her head.

"I... I can't," she said, being then interrupted by the woman. She held Ayana's shoulders and shook them, crying something.

"She want you" the man said.

"But I can't, I'm just a geisha," Ayana said, feeling pity for her caretaker. "Please tell her I have a home and they need me there."

The man translated and the woman looked worried. But, before she said anything back, Ayana had an idea. Her eyes brightened when she looked at the picture the man gave her. She looked at both of them, holding their hands.

"I will find who did this to them," she said. "But first, I have to go back."

Stammering words, the man translated what Ayana said. She went on:

"They will pay for it," she groaned. "But I cannot do this if I don't go back."

They were both silent after the translation was once again done. Ayana now turned her sadness into anger. Her blood boiled. She now had an urge, a purpose.

She got up and went straight to the washroom. She heard the woman going after her. She helped Ayana bathe and dress. Then went on to get her food while Ayana herself packed. She liked how the woman seemed to know exactly what to do. Like their minds worked equally, as if they were the same person, even though they couldn't understand each other.

While putting her belongings inside her case, Ayana separated some money she had with her and put it on her robe. The woman entered with a tray of food and Ayana ate everything in a hurry, realizing how hungry she was. When she finished, she got her luggage and went outside to wait for Taichi, the maid following her. The man was also outside already.

Ayana sat in a bench, arms crossed, impatience dominating her. She knew Taichi would be there soon.

After an undetermined amount of time – Ayana was too immersed in her own thoughts to keep track – Taichi appeared at a distance. Upon seeing him, Ayana went to the man and the maid.

"Listen," she said, taking some of the money out of her robe and giving it to him. "Take this, I insist. And this for you," she said, giving the rest of the money to the woman. "You have to leave this place. And I will make sure what is happening to these girls won't happen again."

She then turned around, before the other two could say anything, and walked in Taichi's direction, luggage in hand.

He seemed surprised in seeing her.

"You're feeling better already?" he asked. Ayana stopped right in front of him.

"I feel anything but better," she said, sharply. "I want to go home."

Taichi had his eyes open wide. He didn't want to discuss with her.

"Uh…" he started. "Okay, come with me."

He walked back to the car behind them, taking Ayana's luggage. She looked back at her maid, her son and the neighbour and waved at them. She would keep her promise.

Taichi arranged a way for Ayana to go home by aeroplane. Using his connections and ways, he got her a ticket and waited with her for the flight. The whole time, they were in dead silence – Ayana was angry and Taichi was uncomfortable.

When the call to her flight arrived, they both got up. Her, to leave. Him, to say goodbye.

"I'm sorry again," he said. "For everything."

He seemed genuine in his words. But Ayana didn't care.

"You should be, but that's not enough," she answered, looking at him dead in the eye. "You ruined my life and I want you out of it."

Taichi lowered his gaze.

"Sorry," he whispered.

"I don't want your apologies, I want you to never look for me again."

With that, she turned around and walked away to the plane, back to her home. To her okiya.

Taichi felt his heart tighten upon seeing her walking further and further away from him.

Was he going to cry, after never doing so?

ƸӜƷ

Mameko was the first one to see Ayana.

She was walking back to the okiya after buying some fruits when a rickshaw stopped at the door and Ayana got out of it. Mameko dropped her bag, in shock.

"Hanako-senpai!" she yelled, smiling and running to hug her friend. She backed away once she realised Ayana didn't hug her back. "Where were you? What happened? Koyuki-san is so worried!"

Ayana didn't look at her.

"We'll talk inside."

With that, they both got in the okiya and Ayana already went after Koyuki-san, Mameko running behind her.

Koyuki-san startled when Ayana opened the door. Upon seeing it was her, the woman got up and walked in Ayana's direction. She hesitated there, looking confused and worried.

At last, she hugged the girl.

"I demand you to tell me what happened," the woman said, sounding more worried than angry. She backed off to look at Ayana's face. It was tired and devastated. "What happened?"

Ayana sat down in front of the woman's desk.

"I found a picture of Hina's house and went to look for it," she started. "Actually, Imamura-senpai was very drunk during the last night we spent together, and begged me to go with him to Manchuria… so I did."

Ayana took a deep breath, closing her eyes. She felt her face warm.

"I ran away and I am sorry, Koyuki-san," she whispered. "But I had to see what happened to Hina, or at least try. So I looked for the house in the photograph… It was a mess. A man I met said the Japanese army took Hina and his niece, and he hasn't seen them since."

Both Koyuki-san and Mameko gasped, covering their mouths with their hands.

"The man saw them coming after Hina and taking her again when she ran away from them," Ayana went on. "I was so overwhelmed with Hina's letter and worried about where she could be, that I… was not careful… I found out I was pregnant."

Ayana stopped to breathe. She didn't imagine talking about this would be so difficult.

"Oh my!" Mameko exclaimed at the same time Koyuki-san crouched in front of Ayana and touched her abdomen.

"It's all right, I don't think it's too late," she said, looking Ayana in the eyes.

Ayana shook her head. Her mind was racing in a million thoughts that consumed her and any little touch disturbed her.

"No, no, no," she responded, closing her eyes to think and

try again. "Listen… I lost the baby," she said. The next words came in a rush. "Imamura-senpai changed everything for the worse, so I told him to never talk to us again."

"What?" Koyuki-san yelled. She grabbed Ayana by the arms. "You *can't* do that, Ayana! He is a man of respect and contacts, people *will* hear about this and it will be bad for *us*!"

Ayana looked at her, not believing what she was hearing. Koyuki-san, while she spoke, shook Ayana's shoulders the entire time. The girl got away from the tight grasp, getting up.

"Is this all you think about?" she yelled. "Reputation? Money?"

Before Koyuki-san reacted, Ayana threw the money and calculator at the woman's desk on the floor, making a loud crashing sound. Mameko screamed.

"Well, *here's* your precious money!" Ayana barked, looking at Koyuki-san with anger. The woman was out of breath, in shock. "Since it is *so* important to you, I am leaving!"

With that, Ayana ran out of the office, hearing Mameko calling for her. She passed by maids in the yard in a rush, and ran to the outside.

She kept running, bumping on people, making vehicles stop and tripping on the floor several times because of her shoes. She didn't look up any moment, the tears never left her face. She just wanted to get away from everything – from the okiya, from the miscarriage, from the evil people.

She suddenly felt two arms grabbing her. She fought against them, thinking it was one of the okiya's maids at first. She didn't have the energy to look up or yell. Soon, she was being dragged to a corner, at the back of a store. Once the arms let go of her, she looked up.

It was Kiyoshi.

"Are you okay?" he asked.

Upon hearing the question, Ayana simply sobbed and hugged her friend, burying her face on his chest. He hugged her back and sat her on the grass. Sitting beside him, she kept her face low, head on his shoulder.

Kiyoshi was worried. First he sees her in a temple and now running like crazy, crying in the middle of the street. Something was off and he needed to ask her about it.

After a while, Ayana did calm down, her sobbing decreasing until she was completely silent.

"Feeling better?" he asked.

"No," Ayana whispered.

Kiyoshi took a deep breath and gently pushed her away.

"I need you to talk to me," he demanded, looking her in the eyes.

Ayana looked down, shy, and started talking. She didn't look up or change her monotone voice.

Kiyoshi got more and more impressed every time Ayana said something. When he thought things couldn't get worse, they actually did. While Ayana wiped tears off her cheeks, he just thought to himself what curse came upon her to go through so much in just very few days.

He could sense a change in her, too. He always thought of her as a calm and happy girl, who didn't worry about many things. Now she looked gloomy and her eyes sparkled with anger. He did not blame her.

Once Ayana was done talking, Kiyoshi let her breathe for a moment. He had an idea that could cheer her up.

"Come with me," he said, getting up and extending his hand. "I know what you need."

Ayana looked confused, but took his hand and got up. She

trusted Kiyoshi.

He took her through the street, letting go of her hand this time. She followed him while he passed on stands of food and scents and greeted people. She knew those people too and bowed to them. Kiyoshi then walked to his stand and took his bike.

"Hanako-chan!" a boy yelled. It was Yasuo. Ayana's heart skipped a beat and she smiled.

"Yasuo-senpai," she exclaimed while he hugged her, his arms feeling stronger than she remembered. She laughed while he backed away from her. "Hello."

"What brings you here?" he asked.

"I am going to take her to our basement," Kiyoshi said. "I want to teach her some techniques."

Ayana frowned.

"Techniques?"

Kiyoshi simply moved his head to the bike.

"Come on in, you will enjoy it."

She then got on the bike, sitting in front of him and he started to pedal while Yasuo waved goodbye.

Ayana closed her eyes while feeling the fresh wind against her face. She felt free. She wished she could just fly away. She wished she could go to a place where she could meet with Hina. She wished she could see her friend.

Involuntarily, Ayana let her arms stretch to the sides, as if they were wings. Kiyoshi held tighter to the wheel and got closer to Ayana so she wouldn't fall. Her hair would occasionally brush against his face and her flower perfume would mix itself in the air. For a moment, Kiyoshi closed his eyes and took a deep breath. He missed her.

Ayana put her arms down again, slowly, fearing she could lose balance. She was laughing, which made Kiyoshi laugh too.

"Here, hold the bike," he said, putting his hands on top of her hands while she rode.

Taking a turn to the left and another to the right after a few metres, Kiyoshi finally stopped. He got out of the bike and offered his hand to help Ayana. She looked up to his house. It was simple, but fairly big, with a side garden where his mother grew vegetables. In front of the white walls of the entrance, his grandmother slept in a chair. Kiyoshi went over to her and adjusted her blanket.

"Come in," he whispered to Ayana, while removing his shoes. She went right after him.

Inside, his mother cooked in the kitchen. The smell of chicken filled the air. Ayana took a deep breath. She was hungry.

"Kiyoshi," his mother called. "You're almost in time for dinner."

Kiyoshi bowed.

"Okaasan, this is my friend, Hanako-chan," he said, pointing at Ayana. She bowed. "Do you remember her?"

Kiyoshi's mother gave a big smile.

"Of course I do! From Koyuki-san's okiya, am I right?"

Ayana smiled.

"Yes, Saito-san."

"Would you like to stay for dinner?" she asked Ayana.

"Yes, that would be great, thank you" said Ayana, bowing again.

Kiyoshi took her by her arm.

"I have to show her something," he said. "We'll come back once the food is ready."

"Where are you taking me?" Ayana asked, once they were at the house's backyard.

Instead of answering, Kiyoshi opened a basement door and

climbed down. Ayana looked in the darkness and saw he turned a lamp on.

"Come on in, I will help you," he said, extending his hand.

Ayana turned around and started going down the stairs. When she looked around, she saw a large room with a lot of space. There were walls with knives and swords and a big mirror on the other side.

Only then she realised.

"This is the club!" she said, laughing. "Right?"

Kiyoshi smiled and nodded.

"We spent a lot of time here," he said. "Frankly, we still do."

Ayana started running around. The room was very big. Its caramel colour wooden floor was covered in powder to prevent slipperiness. Its walls were of wood and washi, in a white colour. That gave the room more of an impression of space than it already had.

On one of the walls, the swords were carefully placed horizontally. It looked as if they were floating.

"Oh my," Ayana whispered, walking to the wall, mesmerized. There were ten swords in two columns of five, all symmetrically positioned under one another and side by side. They were very long, curvy and their cases were of a shiny noir material. Some swords had golden edges, some had silver.

"They are tori-soris," Kiyoshi said. He approached one of them and picked it up. "It's a type of katana, really. More curvy. And here," he took the sword out of its case. The noise made was cold and yet comforting to the ears. "This edge is called o-kissaki. They are very big tips, perfect for cutting."

Ayana brushed her fingers against the silver shiny blade. It was like a mirror.

"What do you cut it with?" she asked.

Kiyoshi stepped aside and started to perform some kicks in the air while holding the katana. He was very agile.

"Pretty much anything," he answered, then smiled while looking at her. "But of course I only cut wood with it."

Ayana smiled.

"Teach me."

"That's why I brought you here," Kiyoshi said, putting the katana down. "A naginata would have been better for you, but I don't have those. And you need to release all your tensions regardless."

He put the katana back in its case and set it aside. Standing in front of Ayana, a few feet away from her, he adopted a serious expression.

"Now stand still and straight," he said, using a deep tone of voice. Ayana obeyed right away, trying not to laugh. "I will teach you the ways of the sword."

She found things funny at first. But, as the hours went by, she let all her anger go towards the kicks and knocks she gave in the air with the katana. She swirled with the blade as if she were dancing with her colourful fans during a presentation in a teahouse.

Kiyoshi's mother interrupted her when opening the basement's door.

"You two stop playing with those and come up to eat."

The soup and the rice were set in front of Ayana as she contemplated it. While she ate slowly, Kiyoshi's parents made small talk with her. They knew Ayana's mother and often took care of her during her pregnancy. They saw Ayana grow up along with their son, the boys and the other girls from the okiya. Ayana felt like they could be a family she would have one day.

After eating, Kiyoshi's father was the first one to disappear into the house. Grandma fell back asleep. Ayana went to help Kiyoshi's mother clean. They both said it wasn't necessary, but Ayana insisted. She didn't want to use katanas while the food sat on her stomach.

"I will be in the basement if you need me," Kiyoshi said.

Once he went outside, Ayana started washing the bowls.

"Thank you for the food, Saito-san," she said. "It was very good."

Kiyoshi's mother smiled.

"That was no problem, my dear, you can come by here anytime you want," she exclaimed. "It has been a while since I haven't seen you or the girls. How's Koyuki-san?"

Ayana looked down and frowned her lips.

"She's doing well…"

Kiyoshi's mother wiped the bowls in silence. Ayana felt tense and anxious for a few minutes that seemed like forever, thinking about what to say next. Until Kiyoshi's mother herself turned to her and touched her shoulder.

"I want to show you something," she said and turned around, walking. Ayana followed her.

They went to the living room, where Ayana saw a few vases with plants in the corners and a few lamps, illuminating the place. At the centre, there was a table with paper and ink. Ayana thought Kiyoshi's mum liked to practise calligraphy until she realised the papers had drawings. She liked to paint animals and plants and also make origami out of them.

"Tell me dear, how are things at the okiya?" the woman asked, while sitting down. Ayana sat in front of her, the table between them.

"They are not so good, honestly," Ayana answered.

She then proceeded to tell the woman everything that had

happened until that moment. She told about how she met Hina, how the trip with Taichi was and what she had found out about her miscarriage and her friend. She told all in more detail than when she told Kiyoshi.

"Kiyoshi-senpai brought me here to destress," Ayana finalised. "With the katanas and all the martial arts." She laughed, softly. His mum did the same.

"Well, I know another way you might find useful," she said, touching her papers. She remained quiet throughout the entire time Ayana was talking, only changing her facial expressions slightly. She felt sorry for the girl.

Ayana looked down at the table while Kiyoshi's mother arranged some blank papers.

"I wanted to be a geisha when I was a little girl," the woman said. "But some things are just not meant for us. I still, however, like art." She smiled, which made Ayana more comfortable.

She extended a brush for Ayana to grab.

"Take this and focus on what you want to draw," she said. "You can also write."

While thinking, Ayana looked at the other drawings and saw a butterfly. She decided to copy it and started drawing her own butterfly. It didn't look as professional as the original drawing, but it was indeed a therapeutically process.

"Not a bad start," Kiyoshi's mother laughed. "Do you like butterflies?"

Ayana shrugged and smiled.

Kiyoshi's mother grabbed her own butterfly drawing.

"They represent beauty, death and new beginnings. You can think of your baby as a butterfly, finally able to flee to the other world."

"Like, the souls turn into butterflies? Some people believe in that?"

Kiyoshi's mother nodded.

"What you are going through right now is a chance to restart, to leave your cocoon" she said. "Accept that your lost child is always watching you. That will make you feel at ease."

Surprisingly, that did comfort Ayana, because it made sense. But it wasn't enough.

"This is not going to stop what is happening," she whispered.

Kiyoshi's mum held her hand.

"My dear, the world and its misfortunes will never stop, and you have to live with it," she whispered. "Your life won't ever be the same because you won't be the same. Come to terms with these changes and you will know what to do to take control of your fate once again."

Kiyoshi's mum smiled to assure Ayana that she would be all right and made an effort to make the girl laugh.

"Do you know how to make origami?" asked Saito-san. "I can teach you."

And so Ayana started playing with the paper. She made a butterfly origami for her child.

"You can sleep here if you want," said Kiyoshi's mother. "But I will make sure to let Koyuki-san know. She must be very worried."

ƐЖЗ

Ayana went back to the basement and watched Kiyoshi do his own things. He helped her get some blankets to sleep and took her upstairs. On the way to his room, Ayana overheard his mother on the phone. She had called the okiya to let them know where she was.

Kiyoshi opened the door to his room and took his own blanket and pillow out to let Ayana replace it with hers. He then wished her a good night and left.

That night, Ayana started overthinking. Her world was now shattered and, although the shock was gone, the scar would remain. She knew she would always live with the emptiness. She just had to figure out how.

The next morning, barely getting any sleep, Ayana got up and got dressed. She folded the bedding nicely and went over to the living room. Nobody was awake yet. Her butterfly painting was still at the table, along with the other drawings. Ayana organized them, leaving hers at the top of the pile. She wrote in it a thank you note to Kiyoshi and his parents. Taking her origami, she put her shoes on and left. She now had a plan in mind.

She was going to head back to the okiya. That was her first step to rebuild the life she knew.

6

The streets were still empty when Ayana made her way to the okiya. The neighbourhood was still waking up. The only sound that could be heard was of her flat zori shoes. Still, she didn't mind it. She was adamant to face any consequences Koyuki-san had for her, without fear.

Upon arriving at the front door of the okiya, Ayana realised it was open – in case she came back. The yard was silent when she crossed it. She peeked in the bathroom, the kitchen and the backyard too – nothing. All the maids were asleep and so were the girls. Ayana walked slowly and quietly through the corridors, checking every room in the house. Koyuki-san's room had its door open but it was empty. Ayana knew where she was.

She went over to the office. The door was fully opened, a weak light illuminating the hallway. Ayana hurried and stood in the middle of the passage. Koyuki-san was at her desk, sipping tea and looking out at nowhere. She had empty eyes.

"I knew you were coming," she whispered and looked up. Ayana walked towards her and sat on the other side of her table, bowing very low.

"Gomenasai, Koyuki-san," Ayana said, head on the floor. "I am sorry for yelling at you and running away. I will never do it again."

"You better not," she answered, still whispering. "But I guess you had to clear your mind. How are you feeling?"

"Not clear yet. I came back not to worry you more or burden

Saito-san too much."

"So…" Koyuki-san put her cup down. "What are we going to do from now on? I can't have you upset for the rest of your life."

Ayana took a deep breath to speak steadily.

"But maybe I will be," she said. "Maybe this changed me for good and it will always leave a scar. I suffered the losses of my mother and grandmother at a very young age," she said, her voice cracking. "And now a child? I don't want to lose anyone again."

"We have to figure out what to do," the woman whispered still.

"I know you said people will hear about what happened, but I don't think so," Ayana started, her voice now stable. "The fact that Imamura-senpai brought me back shows he plans on following my wishes. This incident is worse for him than for us."

"I disagree," Koyuki-san said. "Situations like this are common for us women, and that won't harm his reputation. It will, however, harm ours if word spreads that you left Manchuria in such a mad state."

"But no one knows about it," Ayana snapped back. "I don't understand, Koyuki-san. All people know is that I went with him, as he wished. He was seen going into the room I stayed at every night, for hours. His colleagues knew he had me there."

Koyuki-san took a deep breath. She poured more tea.

"The problem is not abroad, it's here. It's how people will see that you and him do not engage in public appearances together. Especially since many barons are aware that there's a high chance he can be your danna."

Ayana's heart skipped a beat. Her breath stopped.

"What?" she said, the word barely leaving her mouth. "He was going to be my danna?"

Koyuki-san looked at her with tenderness.

"Many men have always shown interest in you and you know that, Ayana-chan. But Imamura-senpai's bid for you was such that your mizuage was the highest. He was really invested in having you. Then you two travelled together. It just wouldn't be a surprise if he actually becomes your patron."

"But what if he doesn't? What if someone else does or if I don't have one at all?"

Ayana was becoming a little desperate. She did not want this situation to drag on, and Koyuki-san knew it.

"It is not logical or acceptable for a geisha like you to not have a danna," she said. "People expect the opposite, and if we show any man can be yours, people will know there's something wrong between you and him."

Ayana felt useless. If that were to happen, her request to Taichi was in vain.

"Is that what you want, okaasan?" she asked, thinking without being able to find a solution. "To have him as my danna for appearances?"

Koyuki-san extended the cup of tea to the girl. Ayana took a sip to calm herself.

"I understand you don't want to see him, and no one needs to know details. It will just be financially good for the okiya. I also have to arrange a danna for Shizu as soon as possible."

Ayana nodded. She knew the business part had to be taken into consideration more than anything else. That's how things always were, and she shouldn't let her private life and emotions affect her household. She was now a geisha and had to support the okiya along with Shizu.

Koyuki-san's okiya, the Hirata house, was highly respected because Koyuki-san herself was very well-known during her youth as a geisha. She inherited the okiya from the previous owner and worked hard to maintain the high reputation the place had. She herself was still very requested at ceremonies and social gatherings. Any novice of hers was the subject of curiosity, her contacts were important, she always had the best services at her feet and her demands were always met. Ayana was raised to honour these standards. Although Koyuki-san had a large amount of apprentices, she only had herself, Shizu and now Ayana to bring money into the place to maintain their high lifestyle, for now.

"But Koyuki-san…" she started. "Imamura-senpai is part of the army. And, when in Manchuria, I saw how they took over the country. And about Hina… she wasn't the only woman to be taken away."

Koyuki-san frowned.

"I don't understand where you want to go with this thought, Ayana-chan."

"I… just don't approve of these things the army is doing and how no one is talking about it. I want to speak against it somehow, but how can I do so if my danna himself is a soldier?"

Koyuki-san closed her eyes and rubbed the top of her nose. She now understood the root of Ayana's frustration. It was much bigger than a pregnancy ceased so early – as if that weren't enough of an issue.

"For everything, there's a solution," she said. "Let's wait for Mameko and Rikiya to wake up. I will start to organize their debut, so they can help with the finances."

Ayana's expression lit up.

"Does that mean I can choose my own patron?"

Koyuki-san looked at her seriously.

"Ayana-chan, you have your own life and are free to have

your own opinions and expressions, but I won't allow you to take this publicly. Imamura-senpai *will* be your danna if he's interested. Showing disapproval towards the army in front of him is not a good idea."

"Let me at least talk to him," Ayana pleaded. "If there is no other option but for him to be my danna, I will accept it and work hard to support the okiya. Koyuki-san, you know that I never felt like I was born to do anything else besides being a geisha. It's in my blood…"

Koyuki-san knew it. She trusted Ayana with her heart.

"We are settled then…" she started talking, but Ayana wasn't done.

"… but I have one condition," Ayana interrupted. Koyuki-san looked at her, intrigued. "Let me ask if he knows about Hina, somehow. I want to know where she is. Only when I have my answers will I feel at ease."

Koyuki-san nodded. She saw no reason to discuss it.

"Fine. Try to take information from him, he owes you that."

ЄЖЗ

One after the other, the maikos were waking up and were surprised to see Ayana was there, and well. Mameko hugged her. Rikiya commented how she thought Ayana had ran away for good and her debut as a geisha would have to come earlier than expected. Shizu had just arrived from a party and approached her, asking what had happened. Ayana told her about Kiyoshi's house, followed by the conversation with Koyuki-san. Rikiya cried about the fact that her debut was indeed going to happen very soon.

Shizu was not Ayana's tutor anymore. Now she was going to

help Rikiya up until she became a geisha. Ayana would give orientation to Mameko. Those were the instructions Koyuki-san gave over breakfast.

"We are going to start the preparations right away," said Koyuki-san. "I feel that you are both ready to take this step, while my other maikos still need more time."

That evening, Koyuki-san informed the entire okiya of her intentions. Rikiya and Mameko were not real names – the girls chose them long ago and were called by them ever since. All they had to do was turn their collars and change their hairstyles to fully become geishas. In the days that followed, the girls prepared themselves to finally debut. During a warm evening, at supper time, Shizu and Rikiya, and Ayana and Mameko performed their bonding erikae ceremony, taking three sips of sake three times. They were now connected as sisters, tutors and apprentices.

Ayana felt good for a moment. Seeing people joking amid the sound of cheerful music and laughs made her forget a little about her troubles. She allowed herself to enjoy that night, knowing she would soon do the same ceremony with Taichi. For that one she already knew she was not feeling festive about.

She went to sleep with Mameko. Singing a lullaby, the girl fell asleep next to her and, looking vulnerable that way, Ayana promised she would protect her little sister at all costs, before giving in to tiredness herself.

The next day, she had a killer headache. The hangover seemed to take on most of the people in the okiya, with the exception of Koyuki-san, always working from early morning until late at night. Ayana heard voices coming from her office. Walking along the corridors, she saw people whispering, and a few maids next to the closed door. They felt a little uneasy seeing Ayana there. She thought she heard someone saying something about a good appearance or a strong voice.

"There's a man in the okiya," one of them said. Men were not allowed in there.

Ayana approached the door to hear. The male voice was muffled, but still familiar.

It was Taichi.

Ayana gasped and ran back to her room, ignoring the confused looks the maids gave her. Mameko was still sleeping. She silently crawled back to bed and pretended to be asleep as well. She planned to not leave her room until Taichi was out of there.

But minutes after, she heard a light knock and the door slide open. She squeezed her eyes shut. Whoever entered the room woke Mameko up. Ayana heard the girl getting up and asking questions while being guided to her own room. The door didn't close. Instead, Ayana felt someone shaking her shoulder. At the same time, the door sled shut.

"Hanako-chan," the voice whispered. It was Taichi. A chill ran over Ayana and she shook, having no choice but to open her eyes and turn around to face him.

He was crouched in front of her, next to her bed. Although serious, for the first time ever, his eyes were calm.

Ayana suddenly became self-conscious of her messy hair and covered herself in the blankets again for Taichi not to see her bare face. He laughed softly.

"I have seen you in worse conditions," he said. "Now, don't be silly and look at me."

Ayana obeyed him. Although much weaker now, she could still feel some tone of command in his voice.

She thought he probably pitied her. And that thought made her embarrassed and angry.

She uncovered her face, leaving only her eyes exposed. Taichi sat down more comfortably.

"Koyuki-san and I had a talk about me being your danna," he started, without looking at her. "So I came here as soon as I could because I will have to travel again, and I don't know when I will be back. We need to have the ceremony later today before I depart."

The thought of him leaving was pleasant to Ayana, but soon replaced by anger. She knew he was going back to Manchuria.

"And then what? Will you return to any of the countries that you helped ruin?" she asked, turning around not to face him.

He took a long breath and let the air go.

"What do you mean?" he asked, in a stone-cold tone.

Ayana thought for a moment. She needed to organize her thoughts amid her bad feelings. Staring at the ceiling, she started to put the words in order.

"I saw what I saw back there. People on the street, dirty and begging for food. And Japanese flags all over town. While the army walked around in their big cars, intimidating everyone. And forcing the locals to change their names and adopt our religion. My friend did that."

"But we had to build our empire," he retaliated. "We conquered China. The West needs to know they can't have everything…"

Ayana sat down and faced him, interrupting whatever he was going to say.

"Taichi!" she exclaimed. "This is wrong. This is all wrong. Using oppression is not the way to do it."

"The stronger wins, that's how the world works, Hanako-chan," he said, as if she was naïve. "You are too young to understand…," he started again.

And again, she interrupted him:

"Conquering with death? With mistreatment? With abuse?" She grabbed his arm so he could look directly in her eyes, and he did, frowning. "I need to know what happened to my friend, Taichi. I need to know where she is."

Her voice tone was changing into a firm one, starting to sound angry. Her nails were carving themselves into Taichi's arm. Her breath started to sound louder.

"Tell me where Hina is!" she pleaded while Taichi looked scared. He slapped her face, making her let go of her grip.

Ayana's face turned to the side due to the impact, and she stood still for a brief second. It was all too fast. She soon felt Taichi's arms around her.

"I am sorry," he whispered. He backed off, holding her face between his hands. He looked at her cheek and kissed it. "I am so sorry," he hugged her again. "Please, Hanako-chan, forgive me. I never laid hands on a woman before, I swear."

Ayana was just surprised. She remained quiet, listening to him. Her face wasn't burning, nor hurting. She slowly backed away from his grip. She saw his arm was bleeding a little, from her own grip.

"Hanako-chan," he called, lifting her chin. He still seemed disturbed. "I am so sorry," he whispered. "I have no idea about what happened to your friend."

Ayana put his hand down.

"A man told me Japanese soldiers took her and his niece away. Do you know anything about that?"

He looked away, and hesitated for what seemed to be a long time.

"Some soldiers are offered… services. If they want, they can go to brothels and there will be women. I assume your friend was taken for this purpose."

He seemed ashamed to know this. Ayana, on the other hand, was mad. She shook her head, not believing it.

"Are you telling me...?" she started, organizing her line of thought, "that my friend was kidnapped... to be a prostitute for Japanese men? Is that it?"

Taichi simply nodded, without looking at her.

Ayana started laughing.

"Koyuki-san will know about this," she said while her laugh stopped, pointing a finger at Taichi. "In fact, the entire okiya and Gion will."

"Hanako-chan..." he started, putting his hands on her shoulders. "I need you to know that I am very sorry. That I am only a man that follows orders. But if I can offer you advice – don't do anything stupid. You don't know what some of those men are capable of. Don't mess with them."

Ayana laughed at his face.

"Taichi, honey... *they* are the ones that don't know what *we* are capable of."

"I am serious," he said. "You can talk to whoever you want, but don't do anything stupid."

"You are not in a place to tell me what to do," she snapped, teeth clenched. "The fact that you will be my danna is proof enough that I already do stupid things..."

"Hanako-chan," he called again, in a stronger voice, interrupting her, "as your danna, I will *protect* you. But I can't do that if you pose yourself against us."

Ayana got his arms away from her.

"I already *am* against you and I don't need your protection," she said, also using a cold tone. "I need you to get out of my room. I will see you later."

Taichi still stood there a few seconds.

"I will try to find out what happened to your friend," he said and got up, leaving.

ƐЖЗ

Later that evening, after supper, Ayana got dressed for the ceremony. Wearing a green kimono with drawings of trees and flowers on its skirt and a dark coloured obi, Ayana looked beautiful and fresh, like spring. Only she felt the opposite of that.

When Taichi arrived, Koyuki-san made a speech on how she hoped those were the first steps for the okiya to prosper for longer and continue to be one of the most important geisha houses in Gion. She then poured the sake cups for both Ayana and Taichi to take three sips from, giving one cup to Ayana, then to Taichi, and repeating the process three times. Shortly after, the okiya was again partying. Taichi was the one that couldn't stay for long. He had a word with Koyuki-san and went to talk to Ayana.

"Hanako-chan, could you come with me, please?" he asked, taking her away from her conversation with other girls. She started walking him towards the exit.

"What is it?" she asked on the way.

He stopped before the door and turned around to look at her. Her kimono was bright, coloured in many different patterns. She looked like a living cherry blossom. He smiled at her and gently touched the cheek he hit earlier.

"I hope you didn't feel pain," he said.

Ayana shook her head.

"Don't worry, it didn't hurt. But never do it again or I will end you."

He laughed, but knew she was serious.

"I will never, I promise," he answered. "But we always bring the worst in each other."

Ayana lowered her gaze.

"That is true."

A brief silence stood between them. Taichi was serious again. "What is your friend's name?"

"I'm not sure… she only went by the name of Hina," Ayana whispered, her voice breaking, "but her address…"

Ayana remembered exactly where she had found the house. Taichi nodded.

"I decided to become your patron to keep supporting you. It is the minimum I can do for… what happened. Now, go back and enjoy our party."

He smiled again, bowing, and left. Ayana rushed back to the okiya and waited until the party was over to talk to Koyuki-san. She wanted to tell about her discoveries and express how she was surprised that he seemed to have had a change of heart for now. Ayana still didn't like him or how he was doing all of this out of pity, but it was better than what she expected of him.

She went back to her circle of friends and continued talking. Occasionally, she tried to coach a tipsy Mameko on styles of dance for her presentation, laughing whenever her now sister fell. Once again, for the second day in a row, she felt as if things were going to be all right after all. For a moment, she thought Taichi had ruined her bittersweet feeling but, at the end, she ended up even better. She couldn't help but create expectations.

When once again the house fell quiet, Ayana knocked at Koyuki-san's door. The woman opened it and seemed to be ready to sleep, which made Ayana feel a little bad for her. It was very early in the morning and she knew Koyuki-san had a few hours before having to return to her duties.

Ayana bowed.

"Sorry, Koyuki-san. Just wanted to let you know that Imamura-senpai and I had a word."

Koyuki-san seemed to pay more attention.

"About Hina?" she asked. Ayana nodded.

"He said he will try his best to find out what happened to her and where she is. I am telling you this because I thought that, depending on what he finds… well… I would want to go back to Manchuria. If he finds her, I want to go see her and I am sure the girls will want too."

Koyuki-san stayed quiet for a while, thinking. She was too tired to object at that moment.

"Ayana-chan, listen… we will have to study this well. I just now pulled the strings to help the okiya's finances, so I can't have all of you out of here at the same time. But I will see what we can do for you to go alone once again. Go sleep now, it has been a crazy couple of days."

Ayana bowed again while the door closed. She then went to her room and laid in bed, not being able to sleep. While she kept thinking about her possible trip, her mind travelled to the time when she met Hina.

ƐЖჳ

Ayana was getting back from school one afternoon. She was training to be a geisha with Shizu's help, who had debuted a couple years back. Her own debut as a geisha was scheduled to be sometime in the near future and she couldn't wait.

Getting back to the okiya, Ayana soon heard Koyuki-san calling her. She ran over to the woman. The house was a fuss that day.

"Go buy some fruits, will you?" she asked, handing some coins.

Ayana bowed and proceeded to run back outside. The maids were busy with Shizu. She had an important gathering to attend that night and needed to get ready, so the maikos were doing the basic chores of the house.

Ayana got to the stores, looking for peaches and apples. While analysing the fruits and getting the good looking ones, she overheard a different voice amid everyone who was talking in the street:

"… no, I want that one. Yes, thank you."

It was feminine and had an interesting accent. Perhaps she wasn't from around there.

"That one, I want that, thank you," Ayana heard again. She turned to see the face. She saw a girl talking to a vendor. It was definitely that girl who was talking. She kept saying something to the seller, he wasn't understanding her. Ayana walked closer, slowly.

"These are all the melons I have," the man said.

"But they are not good," the girl replied. Ayana controlled herself not to laugh and stepped in before the man lost his patience.

"Give me some melons, will you?" Ayana asked and the man did as she said. She started analysing them, as if the girl wasn't there. She then looked at her. "These two are actually good, don't worry."

The girl looked confused. Their eyes locked and Ayana was admired for a second. The girl had different facial features and looked very pretty and delicate. She was definitely not from there.

"Thank you," the girl said, still confused, but took the melons and paid the man. Ayana paid for her own fruits and rushed towards the girl, who was already a little far.

"Wait!" she called, and the girl turned around. Ayana caught up to her. "Where are you from?"

The girl smiled, showing bright teeth.

"I'm from Manchuria, my name is Hina," she said, her accent becoming more apparent.

"Hina?" Ayana asked, confused.

"Yes, that's the Japanese name I was given."

Ayana smiled.

"I was also given one! Hanako."

The girl looked confused again, her straight brows frowning.

"You're not Japanese? But you look Japanese! And you speak good Japanese."

Ayana laughed. Hina was adorable.

"Yes, I am from here. But I'm a geisha, and Hanako is my geisha name. My real name is Ayana."

Hina seemed to understand and smiled again.

"I like Ayana! I will call you Ayana-chan. And you call me Hina-san."

Ayana laughed again.

"Right. And how old are you?"

"I'm sixteen, so I am *san*," Hina smiled, while Ayana laughed hard. She loved how the girl was so innocent.

"But I am seventeen!"

Hina's eyes widened. She was actually shocked.

"Oh," she covered her mouth. "You look so young! You are so pretty!"

"Thank you, Hina-chan, you are very pretty too," said Ayana, blushing.

She then asked Hina what she was doing there. She replied it was her father's work – they had to move to Japan shortly after the Japanese army arrived. Ayana didn't understand very well, but did not ask further questions.

Hina said it had been only a couple of months since she had moved there with her family, and they were learning Japanese. She was buying melons for her mother's cramps. Ayana laughed at the way Hina said things and admired that she was straightforward. While they talked, they kept walking without destination, distracted. None of them were going in the directions of their respective houses.

"What is it that you are again?" Hina asked. It took Ayana a second to understand.

"A geisha," she replied. "I was raised in a geisha house and since then, I train to be one."

"What is that?" Hina asked again.

"It's an entertainer of sorts," Ayana answered. "We learn dance, music, poetry, painting… and so we are hired to socialize with other people in events."

Hina's mouth opened while she exclaimed.

"Oh… that seems fun! Is it difficult?"

"It is, very. But also fun sometimes."

And then, as if having a realization, Ayana gasped and held Hina's arm.

"You should see a dance one day!"

"Your dance?"

"Yes! Or my friends'. You could also go to our okiya one day and see how it is."

"Then we should meet again! I want to see your friends."

They decided to see each other on the coming Sunday morning in front of the ice cream shop. Ayana was going to take Hina to the okiya and show her the kimonos, the makeup, the maikos. She knew they would be delighted with the visit.

At first, Koyuki-san approved, but acted strangely towards Hina. Ayana didn't know, but the woman pitied the girl. She had a sense of what that family might have gone through. That caused Koyuki-san to watch Hina's every step while she visited and, giving her some homemade food, asked that she show up again. Hina went to the okiya many times throughout that year, as she bonded with the girls quickly. Every time she went there, Koyuki-san would give her some food to take home. She grew fond of Hina and a sense of protection grew on her, as well.

Shizu, Mameko and Rikiya would be around Hina all the time, teaching her Japanese, doing her hair in a bun or applying powder on her face. Hina once came over with ribbons her mother gave them. She also showed up with photographs and gave all of them one. Ayana had the picture of a house. Hina told her to visit sometime.

The week after giving the photos, Hina showed up at night. She always went to visit during the day and caught them all by surprise.

"I have to go," she said, in tears.

Back then, Ayana and the others couldn't imagine that was only the beginning.

7

Ayana got out of the rickshaw and went to the teahouse. Koyuki-san had allowed her some days off since she came back from Manchuria, but now it was time to work hard again. That wasn't her first errand since her break was over, but she was still forcing herself to pick up the rhythm of things.

She felt as if the weight of her pain dressed on her each time she put on a kimono, her responsibilities tied themselves up on her hair and her efforts on keeping her mind sane were applied on her face with powder and lipstick.

She got in the room, filled with at least six men and five geishas and two maikos. She knew some of them from other encounters.

She made her best effort to smile.

"Hanako-chan!" one of the men exclaimed. "So good to see you again. Are you feeling all right?"

Ayana bowed. Koyuki-san made sure that whatever was happening wouldn't leave the okiya. Word spread that Ayana simply had a fever.

"Yes, thank you for asking. And how have you been, Tanaka-san?"

"Very good, very good," the gentleman replied. Ayana respected him. He was polite and knew how to have intelligent conversations.

Ayana also greeted the other guests and made small talk with them, followed by drinking games. She did her best to enjoy and have fun at that moment, her last engagement of the day. The conversations varied from movies to politics, then to kimonos, philosophy, life events and so on. Ayana liked those storytellings the most. However, the politics subject interested her at that moment. They talked about the war.

"We sided with Hitler and are going to fight the Americans again," said another man. "We conquered many countries nearby and Germany did the same over in Europe. But I heard our empire needs to be controlled and destroyed."

"These are difficult times to be powerful," said Tanaka-san. He looked over to Ayana and the other women. "Find refuge in the countryside as soon as possible, ladies. We won't be safe much longer."

Then the subject changed once again. But Ayana kept that stuck in her mind – the atrocities that were happening outside of her comfort zone, her bubble that was Gion. Her heart ached thinking about Manchuria, Hina, and the many other women who were suffering the same as her friend did.

She felt nervousness creeping over her. Take refuge? Where? When?

Back to her home, she was startled by a maid who gave her a letter as soon as she got in the okiya.

"For you. It's from abroad."

Ayana teared the envelope in an instant and saw two pieces of paper in it. She opened the first one. Like she expected, it was from Taichi.

Hanako-chan,
All I could gather was information from some fellow soldiers who have been to brothels in other countries. I had to be

honest with them and explain you were not a threat, but someone looking for a friend. I said you just had received suspicious information and wanted to clear things up, for the sake of the empire. They believe you are trying to denounce fake propaganda.

One of my superiors said Hina most likely went to a sort of camp, what we call "comfort stations". I wrote a fake letter in front of him to prove I was reporting to you what he ordered me to: that your friend is still in her home and, whoever said otherwise, is mistaken. I managed to send this letter instead, as you can see. So no one knows I am writing you this. No one knows that I found the neighbour's niece either.

I spoke to her and, although she was very reluctant in front of me, she decided to write you a letter as well. She did not let me open it, but please, read it.

Another thing: a war is slowly waking up, and our country is involved in many battles now. I don't think we will see each other again in this life.

Go to a safe place outside of Gion. Tell the others.

And don't reply. Burn our letters.

Ayana read the letter several times. The thought of never seeing Taichi again didn't bother her. What bothered was the fact that, if they wouldn't see each other anymore, that meant he would be in battle. He could die. For a couple of weeks now, she would see a different kind of agitation in the streets, a sense of urge that wasn't normal. This was all way more serious than she thought at first. The reality of losing everything was slowly hitting her, and what Tanaka-san said at the teahouse resonated in her ears again.

Ayana moved on to the next paper. The writing was less clear and with some errors, but she still managed to understand what the girl wanted to say.

Dear strange girl,
I will be brief with you. I thank you and your friend for saving my life. He is the first good soldier I have met in a long time.

Hina is no longer here. She didn't wake up one day. This is a chapter of my life I want to forget, so I will spare details. Just know that me and Hina went through a lot. At least we had each other. I am blessed to be able to come back home, but I wish she was with me.

I know you are looking for her. I am sad and sorry that you didn't know any of this before.

She was tough and brave the whole time. And she told me about all of you.

We will never speak again, so I will only ask you one thing. Set an altar for her.

And don't ever come back here.

8

Ayana let the water run over her while she just sat there, thinking about how she was going to deliver such news to the girls and Koyuki-san. There was no way she could do this except being direct with them.

She went back to her bedroom in silence, mixing herself with the shadows of the hallway that gloomed as much as she did. As soon as she closed her eyes and images of Hina flowed to her mind, she heard a noise – like someone was flipping through papers. Tense, she turned over to see who it could be, but saw no one. Was she already dreaming?

Instead, there was something floating. Ayana squeezed her eyes to see better. She thought she was imagining, but it was real – the origami she made was flying. Ayana got up slowly and walked closer, in silence. As if the origami could be startled by her sudden moves.

It was wiggling its wings faster and going higher in her room. Until it suddenly dropped on the floor, a loud cracking noise echoing in the small space.

ƐЖƷ

The okiya's fuzz woke Ayana up. It was probably late in the afternoon, judging by the orange sunshine on the floor, spread like a painting. The origami was back to where it had been the night before.

Sitting down, she noticed there was a tray with soup one of the maids must have prepared for her. Ayana ate slowly, but still anxious about having to speak with the others.

She took the tray out and a maid soon showed up to collect it.

"Do I have any appointments today?" Ayana asked. The maid said they had been cancelled.

At that moment, Koyuki-san was passing by in a hurry and grabbed Ayana's arm. The girl startled.

"Tonight," the woman said, in a firm tone, and left.

Walking around the okiya, Ayana noticed none of the girls were there, since they were all busy for the day. Mameko and Rikiya had had their erikae ceremonies combined. Shizu had had hers a couple of months prior and Ayana attended it. Now all four of them had dannas and the house was going to get more money into it. There were rumours other maikos would debut in the near future as well. Things seemed to be moving on, despite everything that was happening.

Ayana went back to her room and stayed there, without leaving. She reserved those hours to read or organize her belongings or sleep. But, as much as she tried to do something to distract herself, she couldn't – Hina would always come back to her memory, not leaving her alone. She would shake Ayana to wake her up, mess her things again or flip through papers.

At some point, Ayana turned her attention to the butterfly origami she had made and thought about the strange dream she had with it. Without thinking much, she picked blank papers and started making more. In an hour, she had made as many as Hina's age. The lives of butterflies are very short. Just like her friend's. Just like her baby's.

A soft knock on the door took her out of her thoughts. She

slid the door and saw a maid.

"Koyuki-san awaits you."

Ayana rushed to the office. Sliding the door open, she saw Mameko and Shizu. As soon as she stepped in, Rikiya was right behind her.

"Hanako-chan," started Koyuki-san. "You said you had something to tell me. So I will let you talk, but be brief. I have something very important to say myself."

Ayana bowed and walked to the centre of the room while Rikiya closed the door and stood next to Shizu. They were all waiting, anxious.

"As you all know me, I am a person who likes to plan everything well," she started, not looking at anyone in particular. "But I didn't plan that trip. I only care about all of you and this okiya, and I want it to prosper. Since I debuted, I swore to follow the rules and cooperate to all decisions Koyuki-san takes, for the sake of this house. That is why I accepted Imamura-senpai as my danna."

She took a deep breath and sighed. She hadn't planned her speech.

"What happened to Hina was sudden, and I needed to see for myself. But having a miscarriage was not on my plans either. I was so shaken by it... and that isn't how I normally am, so I apologize. And I spoke to Imamura-senpai to help us find out what we wanted."

Ayana paused. No one dared to interrupt her. They were all staring at her as if she were a movie. No one blinked. The okiya was in dead silence. The entire time, Ayana had to whisper.

"I went to Manchuria and met a man who was Hina's neighbour. He was the uncle of a friend of hers. He told me the Japanese army had taken both of them somewhere. Imamura-senpai wrote to me saying he found this niece and was able to take her home. She wrote me a letter as well, but I burned both, like he asked me."

"And Hina?" Koyuki-san asked.

"Hina…" Ayana started, her voice cracking. "Is gone."

There was a brief second of silence, where the eyes of each one of them widened and the chests moved up and down fast.

"Gone?" Mameko voiced. "H-how? Where… where did she go?"

Rikiya turned to her with angry, watery eyes.

"For the sake of this place, Mameko!" she yelled. "Hina is dead!"

No one reacted. Mameko simply lowered her head, tears rolling down her eyes. Rikiya put an arm on her shoulder.

"What I don't understand is…" she started. "How we could be so passive throughout this whole thing. We should have worried about Hina long ago and looked for her ourselves, with no help from anyone."

"But Imamura-senpai's help was what got that girl out of the place she was in, and how I found out all of this…" Ayana defended.

But Rikiya was adamant.

"Hanako-senpai, I don't think you understand," she said. "He *abused* you. You went there to entertain him, got drunk and he just went *in* you. We shouldn't normalize this."

"Rikiya-chan, people make mistakes and have a change of heart as well," Koyuki-san intervened, serious.

Rikiya stood up.

"I have nothing against Imamura-senpai. But don't you see? Hanako-senpai is right in not liking the empire," she looked at Ayana. "Yes, we heard everything you and he talked that morning."

Looking back at the group, she proceeded.

"Look what they're doing – using women. Imagine what Hina had to go through… she's dead because of those men. And so is her family."

There was a moment of silence and glances exchanged. Rikiya was right.

"And not only that. The other day, Mameko-chan got dragged around on the floor at this one teahouse by a drunk customer who wanted to see her legs. Shizu-senpai constantly gets harassed by old men as well... And, not long ago, I had to undo my hair and use my kanzashi to stab a man's neck on the street." She stopped to breath. "I am just tired of all this. I don't know about you, but Hina's death is the cherry on top of the cake for me. I had enough."

"Imamura-senpai did seem to have a change of heart," Ayana said. "My miscarriage affected him, I could tell. He also apologized and I accepted his apologizes. But that doesn't change the way I feel about him or what happened to Hina. There are many other girls in the same situation as her."

"I am afraid their situation is going to get even worse," Koyuki-san said. "The demand for such services will increase, now that we are at war."

The girls gasped at the same time and started asking what she meant. Koyuki-san silenced them.

"We attacked the United States this morning, and there are rumours they will retaliate. Today was agitated because everyone is leaving. And you will have to leave as well."

Another wave of silence crossed the room. For a second, Ayana forgot how to breathe.

"But where will we go?" Mameko asked, her voice braking

mid-sentence. This was all more serious than they thought.

"Where are *you* going, Koyuki-san?" Shizu wondered out loud with urgency, holding the woman's hand.

"I don't know. The countryside is the safest option. I personally don't know anyone in those areas, but staying in a big city is dangerous."

"Why can't we stay?" Ayana asked. "We can figure out a way to hide here."

Koyuki-san looked at them with sadness.

"I am closing the okiya."

ҘЖЗ

Ayana went to the garden. It had started to snow. The flakes were swiftly falling, touching her hair, her clothes. She extended her palm. They dissolved as soon as they fell on her hand. Brief. Like a cherry blossom in spring. Brief like Hina's life.

The okiya was unusually quiet. Now she understood why – the maids were already long gone. The maikos were with their families. Ayana didn't have one. She knew Koyuki-san also didn't. The girls, however, had distant relatives. They were Ayana's only hope.

"Hanako-chan," Shizu whispered. Ayana turned to her. Mameko and Rikiya were behind her. "Since becoming the atotori of the house, I lost contact with my family. My siblings were married off and my parents moved in with my grandmother to Hakone. I am sending Koyuki-san to stay with them."

Ayana blinked, confused.

"Is that okay?"

Shizu lowered her gaze.

"Last time I heard, my grandmother was taking care of my

mum, and my dad stopped drinking when I left... Either way, I don't think any of us should go," she said, her voice low. "We have the feeling we should do something about all of this."

"What do you mean?"

Shizu showed her a stack of papers she was holding. They all contained very short messages of how the army was doing atrocities to the people in their colonies. Ayana picked up the papers to study them better.

She looked up to the girls.

"We can get in trouble for this."

"*If* they catch us," Rikiya objected. "I wrote it all. I can just throw it in the air for people to see it."

"In case we *do* get caught," Shizu said. "We can't endanger our families."

"And what have you told them? Wouldn't they just make you go to safety anyways?" Ayana wondered.

Shizu took a deep breath, steam coming out of her mouth. Ayana realised how cold it was.

"I think trying to spread these letters is the minimum we can do. I am not sure if it will have much effect, but I just want to leave once I am finished. I am taking all of you with me."

"Oniisan," Mameko started. "The thing is... I only have a brother, and he's in the army. I don't like to think he might be doing something... horrible. And I can't stop worrying about him. I want to stay, so I can look for him once this all ends. That's why I am also not going. I don't have any family besides him."

"And my family is dysfunctional," said Rikiya. The girls kept looking at her, waiting to hear more, but she simply looked back at them and shrugged. "What? That's all you have to know. I only have this place."

Ayana then realised the same applied to all of them – the

okiya was all they had. Their home. And even that was being taken from them.

Like Rikiya, Ayana was also tired. She had enough of waiting and whining.

"If anyone attacks us, we will fight back," she said, firm. "We won't stop until this stupid war is over."

Mameko looked confused.

"Attack who? How?"

Ayana smiled.

"Pack your things. I know a place we can go."

Heading to her room, Ayana gathered anything that was necessary for her. Before closing the door, she looked over at her bedroom and prayed it would look exactly the same once this all ended.

In five minutes, she was out at the garden again. Koyuki-san was outside, ready to leave. Shizu was talking to her and the driver. She then hugged Ayana and Mameko and Rikiya when they showed up.

"I will see you all soon, hopefully," she said. She got in the rickshaw and headed out. The okiya was now locked, officially closed. There was no sight of Koyuki-san anymore. Ayana felt empty.

She turned to her friends.

"We can go to Kiyoshi's house. He will teach us how to defend ourselves."

"What do you mean?" Shizu asked.

Ayana had started walking, so they all went ahead.

"I slept at his house for a day and he taught me how to use a katana," she said. "I think it will be useful if we all learn it."

While they walked, Rikiya would throw the papers in the air. The streets were a fuss and no one really noticed them. Ayana saw her friend being upfront enough to even hand some of the papers to people on the street, who would just grab them and proceed to walk, or simply ignore her. Shizu stamped some on trees or light poles.

"*Hey*!" they heard a man yelling. He was wearing a uniform. "*Get in the car, now.*"

The girls started running. Ayana could hear steps getting closer and hurried her pace, mixing herself to the crowd. She also heard Rikiya laughing frenetically.

Mameko screamed and they all turned around. A soldier had grabbed her arm.

"What were you doing?" he asked them.

But all the papers were gone. And that was the problem – in such a tense moment, people feared and suspected everyone and everything.

In a matter of seconds, Rikiya hit the man with her bag, strong and fast enough for him to let go of her friend and stumble. Shizu quickly pulled Mameko and they all ran again. The chase came to a stop once there were enough people to block the man's vision for a moment.

They finally got close to Kiyoshi's house, where he was standing outside with Yasuo and Yoshiki. Ayana rushed ahead, to their encounter and surprise.

"Hanako-chan!" Kiyoshi yelled and hugged her. He looked worried. "What are you guys doing here? Where is Koyuki-san?"

"Can we explain inside?" Rikiya intervened. "We are kind of running away from someone."

Ayana looked back and saw the men very distantly. There were many people running in the space between them and the soldiers but, if they stood there, they could easily be found. The group rushed to the basement without further questions.

"We are planning to stay here," Kiyoshi said, showing them an entrance Ayana hadn't seen before.

In a corner of the spacious, bright room, there was a hole on the wall, with stairs leading down to another area of the basement. Voices were coming from there, and Kiyoshi's father emerged. He greeted the girls and rushed upstairs.

"We are moving essentials from this basement and the house down there," Yasuo said. "And we are staying there until this mess is over."

"We can occasionally try to sneak out during emergencies," said Kiyoshi. "You girls should go ahead too, and tell us everything."

The girls went downstairs and saw Kiyoshi's grandmother, Saito-san and Kobayashi-san. They all bowed.

"What brings you girls here?" Saito-san asked.

"Excuse us, Saito-san," Ayana said. "But this is our only option."

Shizu stepped forward.

"Only I have a family, and I sent Koyuki-san to stay with them, on the countryside," she said. "We decided to stay because of our friend."

At that moment, a loud sound took over and the place they were got darker. Yasuo's and Yoshiki's mother lit a lamp. The boys arrived with more belongings, followed by Kiyoshi's father.

"This is all we will need for now," he said. "The house is safely closed and so is the basement."

"The girls are staying here," said Kiyoshi's mother. "They are about to tell us why."

There was a brief silence before Shizu decided to say something. She was the one to first see Hina's letter after all.

"A few years ago we became friends with a girl named Hina,"

she started. "Recently, we got a letter from her where she explained a... dangerous situation she was in. Hanako-chan investigated and we found out that... this friend of ours is... gone."

Kiyoshi's mother looked at Ayana with a sad smile. She knew well how the girl was overwhelmed with it all.

Shizu took a deep breath.

"Koyuki-san also informed us she had to close the okiya for safety, and sent everyone home," she whispered. "So I told her we would all meet her at my family's house. But we agreed," she looked at her friends, "to do something about our friend. We are not really sure what it is yet, but we need to stay."

There was silence. Everyone was taking in the information. It was so resumed. Ayana had taken in so much more.

Rikiya broke the ice.

"I wrote notes about it," she said. "I wrote about what our friend suffered on the hands of the military, which is probably what many others in the territories we took over are going through. So we spread these notes around the streets and someone saw us."

"A soldier grabbed me," whispered Mameko, fast enough before anyone could object. "But Rikiya-senpai saved me. He wanted to get all of us."

"This is dangerous," said Kiyoshi's father, finally, in a deep and serious voice. "Why run such a risk for someone who is already dead?"

Ayana felt upset by his response, but she understood him. She certainly didn't want them to suffer any consequences.

"Saito-san," she bowed. "I suffered great grief because of this situation – we all did. So we felt like people should know, as they could have gone through anything similar. However, we need to defend ourselves," she took a deep breath, organizing her thoughts. "We don't want anything that happened with our friend to happen again to anyone."

"I know my family is safe," Shizu spoke once again. "But we are not, at least not in here. We wanted revenge, and now we need protection."

"We will protect your house," Ayana said. She looked at Kiyoshi. "But we need a little help."

There was silence again before Kiyoshi gestured for them to go upstairs. He opened the passage and kept it open. Ayana and her friends walked out without making out the expressions in the adults' faces.

"So…" he started. The girls were side by side, facing the boys. "We will help you study the blade. Again." He looked at Ayana and blinked.

She smiled and turned to her friends.

"We are not geishas anymore, girls. We have a mission to accomplish now. And, as an ordinary person, I have a name. I want to know your true names as well."

"I heard Koyuki-san calling you by your name," Mameko said, lowering her head. "But I don't remember what it was. We were all… focused on something else."

Ayana smiled at her as a comfort. She knew Mameko was talking about the incident where she yelled at Koyuki-san for the first and last time, and it was a little embarrassing to mention it in front of the others.

"Ayana Takahata," she finally responded.

They all showed some surprise. Mameko specially.

"Yes, that was it!" she exclaimed and put her hand on her chest. "My real name is Maiya Yamaguchi."

"You have beautiful names," Shizu said. "Mine is Sadako

Matsumoto."

"And I am Maki," said Rikiya. "Kioko Maki."

"So… Ayana, Maiya, Sadako and Kioko," said Yoshiki. The girls turned their attention to him and the boys.

"All right then," Kiyoshi clapped. "Shall we start?"

PART II

苦しみ – kurushimi

(suffering)

9

Hanzou laid back on his chair and took a deep breath, pressing the top of his nose bridge. His assistant bowed to him and handed papers as if he wasn't sure if that was the right thing to do or not.

And now, in front of him, there were a pile of twenty or so pamphlets written with all sorts of accusations – quite repetitive ones, he would say.

He laid back to read them again. They were dirty and wet from being thrown on the ground. Some were torn up.

"Hm," he grunted and threw the papers back on his desk, wiping his hands on his trousers. "Were there more?"

"Hai, sir," said the assistant. "A lot of people had them in hand."

"And who was handing them out?"

"Some… girls, sir."

Hanzou thought for a moment.

"Ask the soldier who gave you these to come here," he ordered.

His assistant bowed and left.

Hanzou reached for one of the papers again. Worrying about little girls was the last thing he wanted. He still wondered, however, about the information written down. How did they know about the comfort stations? How had they heard about Manchuria? They were accusing the army of terrible things, but how could they have found this all out?

The Imperial Army was mainly stationed in China and

Mongolia. For these girls to have knowledge of what was going on in the colonies, they had to have been there. He was intrigued. Much of the information was highly confidential, even to some soldiers. Therefore, someone had to give it to them.

His assistant came back, and a young man in his early twenties, tall, with wide shoulders, hair cut short, and wearing a uniform bowed and stood there, waiting.

Hanzou put the papers down and turned them towards the lad. He folded his hands.

"Who gave you these?"

"I saw a group of girls running around with them," the soldier said. "They were stapling them on poles and distributing them to people."

"Do you recall their faces?"

The soldier hesitated.

"They were very young and were dressed in expensive kimonos. Like… geishas."

Hanzou frowned.

"Geishas? You mean to say teenagers that serve tea and sleep with married men simply decided to give us a headache?"

Before the soldier could answer, Hanzou started laughing. He just couldn't resist the idea of little girls causing such problem. But he did get a bit fearful. They had contacts inside the units somehow. And they were not supposed to.

Clearing his throat, Hanzou looked at the soldier.

"Find out who did this," he said, serious once again. "They seem stupid, but, in the wrong hands, can cause a fuss."

"Hai, sir," he said, bowing and leaving with the assistant.

Hanzou reached for his phone. The other line picked up.

"Watanabe-san," Hanzou called. "It's Yamamoto. I have a matter to discuss with you regarding civil disobedience."

"What is it?"

"I will be sending you some sort of... pamphlets your way. They contain information about our comfort stations. It seems they were made by a group of geishas."

"Geishas?"

"These girls were seen distributing them on the streets. Either someone gave the papers to them, or they wrote it all out. One way or another, they had access to our affairs, and may have much more that we do not know yet."

"I will investigate my stations, Yamamoto-san," Watanabe said. "I will also inform Nakamura-san, as soon as I take a look at the papers."

"Please do," said Hanzou, hanging up.

He picked the papers one by one, analysing them once again. If this went on, they would lose everything.

ƐЖЗ

Ayana sipped on her tea again. It had been a week since they were hiding and training; Kiyoshi's mother would cook with whatever supplements her husband got. They would have to leave soon.

Sadako and Yoshiki were practising combat nonstop. Maiya was wiping her katana clean. Yasuo was drawing. He often helped Kioko elaborate on more posters. Ayana had given them all the information she could, based on what the letters had told her. Kioko would write it either in sentences or in the format of a little story – what they believe was Hina's own story. Yasuo would then make drawings or fix her calligraphy. At the end, they looked presentable and ready to be sent out to the public again.

She just didn't want the boys to get any more involved.

"Hey there," Kiyoshi said. Ayana smiled at him. "So... this war, hu."

She laughed. They would constantly hear the panic outside. Nothing was really happening, but everyone was tense.

"Well…" she started. "We are all just waiting for the worst to happen."

"Except it never does," he replied.

But they knew this could end anytime. The food supply was running short, and staying underground for so long was starting to make the whole family uncomfortable.

"Are we doing well in our training?" Ayana asked, looking at Sadako and Yoshiki. They seemed to have rehearsed a dance for several months, so in sync with one another.

Kiyoshi was smiling.

"You guys are doing really well! I am actually impressed."

Ayana didn't smile back. She had the constant feeling this would all come to a bitter end pretty soon.

With that in mind, she turned away from Kiyoshi and walked over to her belongings, ignoring the gaze he gave her. She knelt next to her luggage and started organizing her things. She was always neat and knew she was not going anywhere just yet – but she wanted to be ready, if that were the case. That basement was not going to keep them there much longer. They needed a plan.

She gathered her clothes on her mattress and folded them into the bag, followed by her comb and her creams. She glanced over at the origamis he had made. They were wrinkled and some were a little ripped. She would ruin them more if she kept them unprotected inside her luggage. And she wouldn't want Hina or her baby to be unprotected.

Picking all the origami, she unfolded one by one, pressing them into a paper ball and throwing it aside. She then organized her bedding and went back to where she was, with the girls.

Kioko and Yoshiki seemed to be done with the posters. They

were straightened on a corner on the floor. One was painted red as if it was blood dripping into the drawing of a girl laying on the floor, like the blood belonged to her, and the sentences written by Yoshiki came from the same red ink. The other poster had the drawing of a shadowy man with a disturbing smile on his face. Another was the country's flag, distorted.

"They look good, don't they?" asked Yoshiki.

Ayana looked at him. He seemed so proud of himself, she couldn't help but smile. He was right.

"They will definitely cause the impact we want," she said. "When are you guys going to put them outside?"

"Whenever they dry," he said.

"Aren't you worried about getting caught?"

He shrugged.

"We plan to go out when no one is on the streets, so we should be fine."

Ayana nodded and looked over at the stairs that lead outside. They were all hiding from having to provide for the country. The door to the basement was covered in leaves, and anyone getting out would wait until it was nightfall to do so. Because of that, it was becoming difficult for Saito-san to buy rations for everyone. It was evening and Ayana could see sunlight from the cracks of the door. Kiyoshi's father still hadn't returned.

It was nothing out of the ordinary. But she was worried guards would come down with him any moment and find them.

Ayana walked over to Sadako. She was still practising with Yasuo when she saw Ayana coming.

"What is it?" she asked, focusing on her friend and on Yasuo's katana in a matter of seconds. Her reflexes were sharper than ever.

"I think we should leave," she whispered, once Yasuo

backed off. "We should pack our things and take the posters with us, at night."

Sadako looked around, thinking.

"And why do you say that?"

"We are short on food and if those men find us here, we will put everyone in danger."

Sadako let go a deep breath. She knew Ayana was right.

"But where would we go?"

"I haven't thought of that," Ayana replied, frustrated. "I just worry about their safety."

"There's no point in worrying about anyone's safety if we're not safe either way," Kioko snapped.

"Why are we here, then?" Ayana asked. "We decided to stay rather than being safe in the countryside, didn't we? It was our plan to stay in Kyoto."

"But it was *you* who gave the idea for us to come here," Kioko replied, angry. "And now you want to *leave*? Do we do things when they are convenient for you only?"

Ayana didn't have to look around to see everyone was observing them. She clenched her jaw.

"Don't be ridiculous," she said, her tone of voice high. "We are short on supplies, and Saito-san hasn't even been back yet. Can't you see how serious this is?"

"Ayana-chan," Kiyoshi's mother intervened. "Kioko-chan. We will be fine, and we will leave together *if* we have to. My husband will come back; he always does."

Kioko glanced back at Ayana before turning her back at her. Ayana knew she was not going to sleep well that night. None of them were.

ΣЖЗ

Later, Ayana laid down and fell asleep quicker than she expected. But her eyes opened soon. Everybody was asleep, covered under their blankets on the floor. The dim light next to her showed a silhouette. Was it Saito-san? Ayana lifted her head and looked around her. Saito-san wasn't back yet.

She looked back to the shadow, in the distance, and realised it was too small to be a man. It was one of the girls. She just couldn't tell which one because of the dark.

Ayana got up, feeling extremely cold. The temperature had fallen twenty degrees, at least. She could see smoke coming out of her mouth. She covered herself and walked up to the person upstairs.

"Kioko-chan, is that you?" she asked, since Kioko was the only one laying down more distant from her.

"What?" she heard behind her. Kioko moved on her mattress, sleeping.

Confused, Ayana looked back upstairs, the girl had walked somewhere. She climbed the stairs after her. It wasn't Kioko, but she knew it wasn't Sadako nor Maiya.

In the basement, the girl was with her back to Ayana.

"Are you all right?" Ayana asked. "Do you need help? How did you get in here?"

The girl turned around. It was Hina.

Her face was grey and covered in scratches and blood. Her hair was a bird's nest.

"Why did you leave him?" she asked in a weak, sad voice.

Ayana heard a scream and everything around her went black.

She woke up with Kiyoshi patting her face, gently.

"Ayana-chan, are you okay?"

She looked around, confused. Everyone was knelt next to her.

"You yelled and fainted, woke everybody up," he continued. "What happened?"

Ayana got up, with help.

"Where is your father?"

Kiyoshi was confused.

"He's not back yet, dear," his mother answered. "Don't worry."

"He needs us," she whispered. "He is in danger."

"He said he would take long this time," Kiyoshi said, in a slow tone, as if he was talking to a child. "Let's go sleep now."

Ayana was still processing. She was sure Hina was talking about Kiyoshi's father. But how was she was going to explain this to them – that she saw a ghost?

She sat on her mattress, seeing everyone doing the same. She couldn't go back to sleep, she was too awake now. Hina was giving her a warning and she had to act.

"Sadako-senpai," she whispered. Sadako was laying closer to her.

"What is it, Ayana-chan?"

Ayana leaned closer. She didn't want the others to hear.

"I saw Hina."

Sadako's eyes widened for a second. Ayana felt the eyes of Kioko and Maiya were also on her.

"I don't know what she wanted, but we have to go," Ayana proceeded. "She gave us a warning."

When Sadako opened her mouth to speak, a loud banging interrupted. There were muffed voices outside.

Everybody was up, tense. The basement door opened violently and soldiers went down the stairs in a rush.

"What's happening?" Kiyoshi's mum yelled, with fear.

"There's nothing to worry about, ma'am," a soldier answered, while the others looked around. "Since we are at war, we must make sure our citizens contribute. Now get your things."

Kiyoshi's mother obeyed right away, gathering all she could while the others helped. Ayana backed off even more into the tunnel, holding Maiya's hand. Sadako and Kioko also backed off. If the soldier that saw them was there, it would be over for them.

The men kept walking around, looking at things in an intimidating way and ordering them to get out of the place. Nothing happened. They weren't paying attention to anyone in particular.

Soon, they were all forming a line and climbing out of the basement. Ayana had her bag tied up around her and her katana on her back. Kiyoshi had taught them how to hide it in an outfit, so they managed to get a hold of their swords without being noticed.

Outside, Ayana looked around and saw it was early morning. There were already a lot of people on the streets and a lot of military as well. She could hear the soldier repeating what he said downstairs – that they had to cooperate, that they shouldn't be hiding in a moment like this.

"Get on these cars," he ordered.

They started getting up in the vehicle. Ayana wasn't liking this, and Kiyoshi's dad was still away. If he did come back, he wouldn't know where they would be.

"Let's try to stay together," Sadako whispered to her. She nodded.

Once they were all in the truck, the driver had the order to leave. When the car started, very slowly, Ayana looked up at the house they were in, one last time. There were some men nearby, talking, and one of them looked over. His expression changed, as if he was alert.

"Hey!" he yelled. The car was faster now, but one of the soldiers inside it still manage to look at him. "Stop! I know these girls, stop!"

Maiya gasped.

"It's that soldier that grabbed me," she said. Her voice became high-pitched. "What are we going to do?"

The soldier had reached the car and climbed on it, once again grabbing Maiya by her arm. She yelled.

"Come with me!" he said, pulling her out.

The others started screaming too. It was all happening very fast. Other soldiers were pulling them outside the truck, while the boys and Kiyoshi's mother were grabbing them. One of the soldiers hit Saito-san. She screamed and let go of Ayana, who easily got out of the truck. Kiyoshi tried to stop him, but got punched in the face and his mother screamed again.

The girls were all struggling to let go of those men. They kept saying they were to be questioned for their behaviour, while telling them to stay quiet. But Ayana didn't stop fighting, and she saw the others also didn't.

Sadako was being dragged. Yoshiki called for her, getting out of the truck and ready to stop the men who were holding her. Maiya wasn't strong enough to resist anymore. Ayana stopped for a second, to process everything. It was all a mess of screams and kicks happening so fast and yet, so slow. The car had stopped, but the passengers were not allowed out.

Ayana's eyes locked with Kiyoshi's. He was doing his best to get to her, but she hoped he could see she wanted him not to. Her eyes were a mix of warning and call for help. She wanted his support, but didn't want him to get hurt.

Her focus switched quickly when a loud scream of pain

came from a male voice. Everyone looked to see a hurt soldier on the floor, blood on his uniform. Standing, Kioko looked at him with an unsteady breath, holding her katana, hands trembling. It caught everyone by surprise.

In that same second, Ayana exchanged looks with the other two. Taking advantage of the distraction, they got rid of the soldiers' grips and took their katanas out as well, standing next to Kioko. The men were still careful around them. One of them gave a small step closer to Maiya. They could jump on them at any time. And they would either succeed or be injured, but Ayana didn't want to hurt anyone.

"Run!" Kiyoshi screamed, and Ayana looked in his direction. It seemed to take everyone out of the shock.

Kiyoshi then took a deep breath and yelled with all his might: "*Run for your lives*!"

Before he finished the sentence, Ayana and the others had already taken off, without looking back.

10

Kioko was still in shock.

"I killed a man," she whispered, hugging her knees and bouncing back and forth on the sandy ground. "I killed a man."

They were in a small compound of trees, not far from the city. They had managed to escape from the soldiers thanks to the crowded streets. Supporting her back against the thick trunk of a tree, Ayana couldn't stop thinking what would be of Kiyoshi and the others.

"We have to get out of here right now," urged Sadako. "They will find us."

Ayana kept looking around for a direction. They stopped for Kioko to calm down, Maiya comforting her.

They had no choice but to travel only with the clothes covering their bodies and swords, now that their belongings had remained in the vehicle with everybody else – including the pamphlets they had made. Ayana knew Kyoto was dangerous for them. They had to be constantly on the move from now on.

This thought scared her. As fast as that, their lives changed forever. She had always imagined a quiet one, living in the okiya until retirement, marrying someone and building a family. And now it seemed like her life was going to be the opposite of that.

"Girls," she exclaimed, getting their attention. "Let's wait for the night to come. If it's dark, no one will be able to see us."

"But why would we do that?" Maiya asked.

"We have to keep running away, now that those men

probably confiscated our bags… they might have seen our pamphlets and, if they find us, we are going to be taken to a factory, for sure," she said, analysing her robes and removing any piece that was too colourful. "Let's all dress up discreetly, so we are not seen during the night or call attention during the day."

"Why don't we just risk staying in the okiya?" Maiya asked, grabbing onto her own dark robe.

"If anyone, or even the army, breaks in there, we can't be seen," Ayana explained, tying her dress up.

"I don't think we should go to the okiya either," Sadako said. "There's too many people around and we won't exactly mix in the crowd, because of the swords… should we try to hide our weapons better?"

Tying the katanas in their dresses and covering them with the robes, the girls walked into the crowd, trying to call as little attention to themselves as possible. It worked because of their kimonos – they were wearing dark cotton pants and shoes that closed at the front, with black silk robes and obis on top, covering everything.

"We should try to buy supplies," Sadako said, looking at the crowd. "Since everything else we had is now on that truck."

There were a lot of shoppers yelling like crazy to get rid of their stocks. The girls avoided any stand that had a soldier buying something. Little by little, they were able to buy some food.

"How much for this?" a voice echoed behind Ayana and she felt a light weight on her back. She turned around immediately, holding her katana tightly. Some people around her stopped to stare, in surprised silence.

The man behind her put his hands up, grinning.

"I just want to know what you'd like for this," he said. "I have a lot of money. I can give it to you if you hand me your sword."

Ayana narrowed her eyes.

"No."

The man chuckled.

"I can give you a lot," he said, taking coins out of his pocket. People started whispering. Ayana maintained herself firm. She feared anyone from the army could come up to them if this dragged itself longer.

The man's expression changed and he started walking towards Ayana, saying something about taking her weapon by force. At that moment, Kioko came behind him and put her katana on his neck. People gasped.

"Give me your money," she whispered to him. "Or I will cut your throat open."

The man's eyes were as wide as they could be and he started to stutter, giving Kioko his little pocket bag. Once she removed her arm from around him, he ran away.

"Let's go," she said, and they all walked away in a rush, ignoring the stares. Ayana was sure the people would spread gossip about this incident in no time, including the man. They had to get out of there.

"Kioko-chan, give me this bag," Sadako said, once the other two caught up to her, and Kioko did as told. Sadako then got her own coins and put inside the bag as well. "Ayana-chan and Maiya-chan, put your money here."

They did and Sadako then tied the little bag up, putting it safely inside her robe. She was carrying a bigger bag as well, with grains of rice.

"Girls..." Kioko started. They looked at her, and only then Ayana realised she was holding on to some papers. She unfolded them slightly and they could see the posters she had made with

Yasuo. "I just realised I still have very few of the posters with me. We can put them up at night."

Ayana felt her spine shiver. She was nervous and anxious, but also excited. That's what it felt like to do what was forbidden, she thought.

"That's great, Kioko-chan," said Sadako. "Now let's find a place to eat."

They kept walking until there weren't so many people on the streets anymore, and it was pitch dark. Occasionally, they would hide in a corner so military cars wouldn't see them. Ayana thanked the black clothes they were wearing.

The girls got to a small, simple neighbourhood. It was quiet and deserted. Ayana felt they should stay there for the night, somehow.

"Sadako-senpai," Ayana called. She was looking at a little house with a chimney. "We have to find another way to travel around soon, but look," she gestured her head to the house and Sadako looked. "It seems there's someone home."

Sadako nodded and started to approach the place, slowly. Kioko already had her hand on her sword. They were all walking with care, trying their best not to be noticed or heard.

"You don't need to knock."

The deep voice vibrated through Ayana's spine, sending shivers. The girls turned around to find a man as old as Saito-san, dressed in a dark blue robe and carrying a pottery jar.

He looked back at them with stableness, serenity. Waiting for them. His aura was serious and warm.

Sadako smiled and bowed.

"Sir, we have some rice, but nowhere to cook it. If you please let us in, we will share it with you."

The man continued to stare at them for a couple of seconds

until he suddenly walked forward, to the door. The girls stumbled to the side to let him through.

"What brings you girls to this area?" he asked, facing the door. "I can see you are not from here."

"We are geishas," Sadako answered. "From the Hirata okiya."

The old man nodded. He opened the door and got in the house, leaving it open.

"I see… and you all didn't go stay with your families?"

The girls looked at one another, not knowing what to say. Ayana felt like she should tell their story.

"It's complicated," she answered. "We decided to stay because of a friend. We want to know what happened to her."

"*Did* something happen to her?" the old man asked. The girls again looked at one another. Ayana lowered her eyes.

"She's gone," Kioko answered. "We tried to gather some information on where she was because of a letter she sent us."

While they talked, the man walked around in his house, as if he were organizing his belongings with no rush. He removed a cloth from the top of a table, taking something dark and long out of it.

He then revealed a katana. Ayana held her breath. How did he know they had swords? Was he going to attack them?

"My father was a part of one of the last samurai generations," the old man said. "I know you young girls probably only have a very basic idea of what you are doing, but I learned a great deal from my father."

The girls looked at one another in shock. The man adjusted himself before getting up.

"Come in. Let's have some rice."

Hesitantly, they walked inside, one by one. Then Ayana could see – while indoors, the man had set a table for them to eat.

"Remove your swords," he said. "If you don't want anyone to see them, don't dress your robes so tightly."

Putting their arms over their heads, the girls slowly slid the katanas up and out of their clothes.

The man looked at each one of them attentively. Studying them.

"I will teach you how to hide it properly, and I will teach you other things as well," he said, his voice reverberating in the small space. "But now, you need nourishment."

He took the bag from Sadako and started to prepare what he needed. The girls sat in silence and did not say anything for a while.

The sweet smell of the spices came up, filling the air and Ayana's lungs with warmth. She closed her eyes and took a deep breath.

"There are eight virtues a samurai must follow," the man explained, while putting rice and tofu in each of the bowls. "To know what is fair, how to act with strength and patience, how to collaborate, to be honest, responsible and loyal."

He sat in front of the girls, giving ohashis to each one of them while saying the words:

"Justice, courage, compassion, respect, integrity, honour, loyalty and self-control," he said, putting the last two ohashis down on Kioko's side. "I am an experienced swordsman. I will guide you through it."

Ayana held her two ohashis. He placed them down while telling her to be just and brave. He had assigned two virtues to each of them. She looked at him, drinking his soup with no rush. Somehow, she could tell he knew exactly who they were and what they needed.

"*Argh*!"

"Ito-senpai," said one of the guards. "What are you going to do?"

Akemi finished drinking the alcohol he had poured in his wound while a nurse wrapped gauze on his chest.

"I… am going to find that girl," he whispered, putting the bottle aside. "She tried to kill me..."

At that moment, the doors to the room they were in opened and another soldier got in.

"Yamamoto-san wants us in his office."

The other men got up and went ahead. Inside the office, Yamamoto-san was on the phone, finishing a call. The men waited.

"Yes, new ones have emerged," he was saying. "I will ask now. Goodbye."

Hanzou hung up the phone and turned his attention to his men. Looking down at his table, he pushed papers in the direction of the soldiers, and sat down.

The men approached and looked at what he had showed. Long, yellow papers had red drawings in them, with written things in a very small calligraphy. The red ink reminded Akemi of his own blood on the ground.

It had only been a day since he had gotten hurt, but it felt more like a few hours. His wound wasn't going to show any signs of healing anytime soon and he had to constantly change his bandage. He could still feel the cold blade cutting through his flesh. Those girls were stronger than they seemed to even know.

"These contain information on our units in Manchuria," Hanzou said. "Someone was there and passed it along to a group of girls. I believe you all encountered them in the city."

He gazed over at Akemi. The soldier simply nodded.

"We are still investigating how they got their hands on this," Hanzou continued. "Meanwhile, I want you all to find them and bring them to me."

"Hai!" the men said in unison, saluting and leaving.

Akemi was now more determined than ever.

He went back to the room he shared with his companions. The best idea was to go around undercover. And they'd have to start it right away.

"Boys, there's no way those girls went far in this weather. We have to stay unnoticed to catch them," he voiced, standing against a table, facing his friends. Some of them were sitting on their beds and some were already packing. But they were all paying attention to Akemi, knowing they had a difficult mission to accomplish.

Akemi grinned.

"For the empire."

꒰Ж꒱

Taichi ran to his officer's tent. Regaining his posture and adjusting himself, he entered in the spacious place, composed of nothing but a desk with a chair and a table on the side. Kyo was finishing his lunch.

Taichi bowed.

"I was called here, Watanabe-san," he started. "Seemed urgent."

Kyo simply nodded and continued to chew his food.

"I… heard some things," he said, drinking some water. "Don't get me wrong, boy. But there are some issues happening right now, and I will need you to give me some honest answers."

"Hai, sir," Taichi responded, not realizing what it could possibly be. "Anything."

Kyo stood up from his chair.

"I want to know about the geisha you wrote that letter to."

For a brief second, Taichi skipped a heartbeat.

Kyo proceeded.

"A group of geishas are spreading confidential information on our comfort stations," he continued. "Tell me, Imamura-kun... what do you know about that?"

Taichi started sweating cold. Hanako was in trouble.

And it was all his fault.

11

Kiyoshi wiped sweat out of his forehead for the millionth time that day. He then proceeded to clean the firearm, laying it on his table.

It had been weeks since he and his family were forced out of the basement. Now, his mother and Kobayashi-san alternated between working and taking care of his grandmother. Yasuo and Yoshiki were with him every day, the whole day, making guns.

And still, no news from his father.

Kiyoshi was now sure he was dead. He didn't dare talk about it with his mother. She still had hopes he was also in a factory, somewhere.

He didn't know anything about the girls, either – he did see the posters Yoshiki had made on the floor in the middle of the street or in walls next to houses. They had been taken down and he hasn't seen any new ones, but he knew word of the crimes the army was committing spread little, as if they were what-ifs. People were just too afraid.

"Do you think they are still in Kyoto?" Yasuo asked, as if he could read Kiyoshi's mind. The whole time, they spoke whispering.

"Something tells me they aren't," he answered. "We should just try to find my father."

"And we will." Yasuo looked at him. "But they could help us." The boy turned to his friend. "Also, I am honestly worried about them. Very worried."

"Me too," Kiyoshi said. "But we got our plan figured out, so let's just go with it. I trust they can take care of themselves."

"I don't know," Yoshiki spoke. He was awfully quiet since they got to the factory. "I haven't seen any posters. I mean, they could have just ran out of paper, but still… maybe they were caught."

Kiyoshi pressed his lips. He didn't like to think about it. First his father and then Ayana disappearing was a heavy burden for him.

"If we do as we planned, then we might find a way to get a lead on them, but we need to do it in parts," he said. "And the first one is to find my father."

The other two agreed. They were getting their mothers and running away to Osaka – it was a big city, and they could hide in another factory. If they kept on the move, they could get away from the soldiers that threw them in that truck. Maybe they could even go back home, to the basement.

It worried him that Ayana was right all along, and he didn't believe her. And now, he had no idea where she was.

Soon, they would have to enlist in the army and stay on reserve until further notice. It had come to Kiyoshi's knowledge that it had been a while since their country had joined the war, and the patriotic sentiment was fervent among the people. The boys would often see children on their way to school shouting excitedly about their duty to their motherland.

Kiyoshi wanted to contribute – people needed protection. However, he couldn't think of dying for a cause without having his father and Ayana by his side. He was trying his best to stay focused on his mission.

"Listen," Yasuo whispered. "First thing we have to do is take our mothers to my house. They already checked your place,

Kiyoshi-senpai, and they could do it again."

"We still have to see if my father is there," Kiyoshi replied. "I thought our plan was to go back to my basement."

"It will be better this way," Yoshiki replied. "We will check for your father, and we will probably be fine. Think about it – there's no suspicion under us anymore, now that the girls are missing... regardless of them being caught or not."

"These men probably think they're dead or that they forced us into hiding them, too" Yasuo went on. Kiyoshi felt a shiver down his spine. "It's like… their structure is falling apart."

"You're right," Kiyoshi replied. "They are so focused on getting people to enlist, they don't have an eye on us anymore. There's a lot going on right now."

Kiyoshi turned his body to his friends and talked lower:

"I am sure they are still trying to find the girls, if they haven't already," he said. "The posters are gone, but people still talk about it."

"It's probably a secret mission of sorts," Yasuo agreed.

"That's what we have to find out," Yoshiki said, looking over his shoulder. "We will leave our mothers at our house, they will be safe there. And then we can look for Saito-san and the girls… even if we have to go overseas. Going abroad could help us understand better what the girls were talking about that friend of theirs."

Kiyoshi thought for a moment. Travelling would only be useful if they could help the girls in a situation similar to the one Hina was in.

"No, the girls are here," he said. "We have to go to Osaka and help them from there, somehow. If we are to be sent away… then we better start to work now."

Kiyoshi looked firmly at the other two.

"As soon as we are done with this, we are running away."

ΣЖЗ

Sensei was always up before the Sun. Ayana would wake with the sound of his movements, eyes fully opened, mind racing. His routine was predictable and reliable. It was as if she were connected to him, somehow. He moved, she moved.

She was always the first one to follow him outside of the house and up to a hill on the backyard. And he always knew she was following him, even though she was silent.

He would sit on the grass and meditate until all the girls were around him. One by one, they would close their eyes and take deep breaths as well. Meditating helped them concentrate before training.

Ayana's thoughts would always drift back to Hina. She would feel the sweet smell of incense from the corridors in the okiya and see her friend at the very end of it, illuminated by the sunlight. Or she would be at a teahouse, sitting in a corner, sipping her drink. She would be kneeling next to Ayana's bed, comforting her while the maid braided her hair and Taichi stood at a distance.

It didn't matter where Ayana saw herself, Hina was always present. Always starring at her with kind eyes. Always standing next to her warmly.

Ayana's mind would drift far away each time. After all, Hina's death marked the beginning of her new and turbulent life.

Sensei would then stand up, making slow and steady arm movements for balance. He did that only when they were all together, never before. Every time he turned around, all four of the geishas would be waiting for him, with their eyes closed, legs folded, hands on legs.

"Control your mind and you control your body," his voice would reverberate. The girls repeated the sentence in whispers, as a reminder.

Every morning was the same.

Ayana always started her training by holding her sword firmly in front of her face, with one leg bent and the other extended behind her. Sensei would gently put his hand on her shoulder.

"Your posture is getting better by the day," he'd say. "Just have a better focus on defending your body."

He would back off from her and, in a sudden move, throw rocks at her direction. With roughness, Ayana would cut right through every obstacle Sensei presented to her. Strength and dedication came out of her body as sweat.

Sensei taught the girls difficulties were blessings in disguise.

They learned how to hold the katanas firmly and wave it without harm. They learned how to strike attacks and dodge them. Paired with one another, they hit their blades together, creating sparkles. Each twist and turn was followed by grunts and sharp metal sounds.

They learned hand to hand combat. How to punch, how to kick, how to roll, how to press. How to hurt. How to kill. With dolls made of wood and leaves, the girls would hit with their fists, ankles and swords. Cracking the heads, perforating the thorax, cutting the arms or legs.

They ran long distances in the extreme heat and the extreme cold. The scalding summer and human sweat were replaced by the strong blows of wind of autumn, making the bodies of the girls shiver, even when fighting.

They cried from pain and tiredness when they couldn't hit

and run any longer. They screamed with frustration every time they couldn't move on. They laughed from relief once they completed an impossible task. They screamed with excitement for their advancement. They fell and got up again and again. That was their lesson.

The enemy is just a fear you want to overcome.

The martial art allows you to make peace with the adversary.

The meditation is to keep you sane, safe and sound.

Control your mind and you control your body.

This routine repeated itself every day.

The girls were laying down on the soft grass, a light layer of snow covering them. The sunset was pink.

"Why do you guys think Sensei is helping us?" Kioko asked. She brushed her fingers against a snowflake.

It had been three months since they were living with the old man. And, in that short amount of time, they were able to grow in an inspiring way. The girls had their lives changed without having anything to give back to him.

"Maybe he's lonely," Maiya replied. "But I'm glad. Otherwise, we would never be here."

Ayana looked at the horizon. That couldn't be the only reason.

"What do you guys think his name is?" she asked.

The girls went silent, thinking. That was a question they always felt the need to ask, but never had the courage to do so.

Sadako was the first one to speak.

"One thing we cannot deny," the others looked at her. "He made the four of us into one. We will always be together now."

Ayana chuckled, resting her head next to Sadako's shoulder. No one was going to break them apart, ever.

₹Ж₃

Saito-san wanted to go home. He couldn't answer any question anymore.

"I am sorry," he whispered. "I really don't know what to say."

The young soldier in front of him wasn't pleased either. He looked tired and angry, dark circles placed under his eyes and sweat shining on his forehead.

He walked from one side of the room to another, slowly.

"Getting any information from this old man won't take us anywhere, Akemi-senpai," said another soldier.

Akemi knew it, but he was certain he had seen the man with the girls and some young boys all together. Before they were caught and placed in that truck. Before he was injured.

And now that man was saying he had no idea who they were talking about.

"He's lying," he whispered under his breath, not caring if his friend heard or not. "We got those boys already," he grinned as the man's eyes went wide. "We just need to know where the geishas are."

Saito-san started sweating cold.

"I-I will tell you everything," he pleaded, hands shaking. "But please, don't hurt my boy..."

Akemi started laughing, whining once his wound hurt, while the old man mumbled about whatever it was those girls had told him. They were indeed on the run, spreading rumours around. The man went ahead in detail, explaining exactly what was being written in each poster he had seen. Often times he emphasized how he and his family did not take an active part in it.

"See, sir... that's where you are wrong," Akemi replied, frowning. "You didn't denounce them – you simply let them make their mistakes. I am sorry but I can't let you go unpunished for this."

As Akemi left the room, the man's screams got more and more muffled until they were completely ceased, eventually.

He still wanted to interrogate the man's son, but now he at least had a lead – the geishas probably had headed south. He needed to get a vehicle and send some men after them…

Such thoughts were interrupted when Akemi almost bumped into something – someone.

"Imamura-senpai," he called. Imamura looked worried, but he didn't care. They were never close. "I didn't know you were back, my friend. Would you like to help me on a mission?"

Taichi pressed his lips.

"I know what you are up to, Akemi," he whispered. "I already did my part. I don't answer to you."

Akemi grinned, putting his hand on Taichi's shoulder.

"You can fool Watanabe-san all you want, but you can't fool me," he said, in a playful tone. "I know you have a thing for geishas."

Taichi turned to walk away, while still hearing Akemi speak louder:

"My superior authorized me to go after them!" he said, in a false tone of enthusiasm. "I will find that girl you love so much, and I will end her before going after you!"

While Taichi hurried his steps, he heard Akemi's vibrating laugh.

Watanabe-san let him go, but didn't make it easy for him – it wasn't easy, after all, to prove his innocence when he had none. He had a mission now – go back to Kyoto and fix this himself.

Through another door, he entered the room Akemi was in only minutes ago. There were other three men present, one of them standing still on a chair, blood staining his coat.

"He was being interrogated regarding the geishas," one of the men informed.

Taichi frowned.

"And what happened, exactly?"

"The geishas were seen living under his basement. We took him in for investigation."

Taichi was observing the man. His face, now pale, still had a frown. His eyes were still open, in shock. He wasn't familiar.

"Ito-kun did this?" he asked, not minding that he was sounding informal. Before the soldier could answer, he turned to him. "Where are the geishas?"

"Ito-senpai is going to look for them, sir. They were seen trying to run away."

"They are still here in Kyoto," the other soldier in the room replied. "Ito-senpai is preparing to send some men after them."

Taichi nodded. The information they gave was the same Akemi had just told him – he wasn't bluffing.

"I see. What is this man's name?" he asked, taking a notebook out of his pocket. "Give me all the information you can about him."

Taichi's blood was boiling. He was in a race he wasn't sure he could win.

12

"You are ready."

That morning, Ayana woke up as if she never slept, only to see Sensei sitting in the living room with his legs folded, hands on his legs.

The girls were waking up and getting the same surprise of seeing him indoors and not on the field.

"Sensei?" Sadako whispered. She wanted to know what they all wanted to know, but couldn't find the words for it. What did he mean? Was it over?

Sensei took a deep breath before looking attentively at each one of them.

"One night, I saw a young girl meditating with me," he started. "She said I was to receive a very important visit from a group of geishas... and you knocked at my door not long after. I am sure she isn't from this world."

Ayana's heart stopped. She looked over to the others. They were all startled.

He had seen Hina.

"I know the cause you fight for, and I have nothing more to teach you," he continued, getting up and heading to the door. "Each one of you accomplished the virtues you have to. Now, go accomplish your victory."

Sensei had a warm smile on him. He had never smiled before in the months they stayed together.

"It was gratifying for me to see all four of you grow," he said, a tranquil echo coming from his voice. "I will always pray for your safety, my warriors. My bugeishas."

Maiya was the first one to get up and give him a hug.

Ayana knew he was right. She had justice and courage from the beginning. Maiya overflowed compassion and respect for others. Sadako possessed integrity and honour to her duties. Kioko accomplished her now developed self-control and, most of all, her abundant loyalty to her friends. All because of Hina.

One by one, they embraced Sensei in a goodbye that would be eternal. They never knew his name – and didn't plan to ask.

Ayana was sure he was an angel.

ƐЖƷ

The truck rocked once again, startling Ayana. Sadako was the only one awake among them. Ayana looked around, seeing it was getting darker by the minute. Snowflakes fell on her hair and stayed there, like a tiara.

"Where are we?" she asked. Maiya started rubbing her eyes.

"Ayabe," Sadako whispered. "We need to think about how to get to Kasai."

Ayana nodded. Once the posters Yoshiki made ended, they then realised there was nothing more they could do – it was impossible to spread any messages on the conditions they were in. So they decided it was time to go after Sadako's family and Koyuki-san in Kasai.

She felt bad about it. She didn't know where Kiyoshi and the boys were, and specially his father. Ayana still remembered her dream with Hina – the question she made was still very vivid.

Why did you leave him?

Ayana was sure she was referring to Saito-san.

"We will have to jump soon," said Sadako, taking Ayana out of her thoughts. Kioko now was also awake.

The truck driver had no idea they were getting a ride with him. That was how they have been moving around for the past weeks – always hiding in the shadows, looking over their shoulders, trying to find ways to get to their destination without being lost. The truck they were at seemed to be the only one worth hopping on.

Slowly and one by one, they jumped and ran away from the vehicle, so the driver wouldn't notice them. The snow made it a little difficult to walk.

"Girls, look for movement and light anywhere," said Sadako. "It's cold. We should find a warm place to stay for the night."

"But how are we going to pay?" Maiya asked. "We don't have enough money."

"We are at war," Sadako answered. "I assume things will change a little."

After a few minutes and passing houses, the girls saw a bigger establishment, in which the lights were on and loud laughs could be heard. They rushed their step to get in there. Closer to it, Ayana could see it was an izakaya.

The girls sat on a table in a dark corner, successfully not calling any attention to themselves. Their black kimonos were really doing their job, Ayana thought.

"I will talk to one of the hosts and ask if we can have a room," Sadako said. She got up and left, walking towards a young man who was pouring drinks. Ayana looked around. Kioko was doing the same as her, although Maiya was barely able to keep her eyes open.

There was a big table in an enlightened corner with a dozen men – the laughs they heard outside came from them. There was another table, with three young couples. They seemed to be from around, their postures comfortable as if they were familiar with that place. There was a man alone, smoking, wearing a hat. Other tables were also packed with more men and women that did not call any special attention to Ayana, since they were far and she herself was starting to feel sleepy.

Ayana drifted for what seemed to be a brief second. She quickly lifted her head up again, realizing Sadako did not return to the table. Maiya still had her head down, but Kioko was looking around. She seemed nervous.

"Where is Sadako-senpai?" Ayana asked. Kioko shook her head.

"I don't know, I only saw her going to talk to the staff, but he's not around."

Ayana thought that, perhaps, the young man went to show Sadako a room, but something wasn't right. She looked around again and everything seemed the same, as she had just lowered her head for a couple of minutes. But then her eyes locked on a corner of the bar. The lad Sadako had spoken with was cleaning a table. The table the cigarette man was sitting in not long ago.

Ayana got up to go outside. Kioko asked where she was going, rushing to wake Maiya up, and soon they were both right behind Ayana.

Outside was dark, just the faint light from the place illuminating the entrance. Ayana saw footprints leading to the left of the izakaya. She rushed her step, hand behind on her back, touching her katana. She slowly took it out, noticing Kioko and Maiya were doing the same. In a very low volume, voices could be heard.

"Do you guys hear that?" Ayana whispered, just to make sure. Kioko and Maiya whispered back, confirming what she suspected. The sounds were inaudible.

Kioko went ahead of Ayana, turning the corner of the place, with her katana out. Not far from them, they saw Sadako with someone, struggling to get away from a grip. She was standing in a way that she couldn't take her sword to defend herself. Ayana narrowed her eyes and noticed it was the cigarette man. He was holding Sadako's arms down and dragging her in the snow.

"Let go of me!" she screamed, moving violently. Ayana noticed that, eventually, her friend would be able to release herself. But until then, she needed help.

Ayana rushed in their direction, Kioko already ahead of her, yelling, her sword in the air. The man stopped and looked at them, quickly throwing Sadako in front of him. At the last second, Kioko put her katana down, her body weight shocking against Sadako's. Both girls fell down.

At that point, Ayana and Maiya had already stood each one on each side of the man, swords out. He then lifted Sadako up and held her tighter against him, putting a gun on her head, scaring the girls.

"Don't make any sudden moves," he said, in a rustic voice. "Or she dies."

They were all holding their breaths. Ayana was close to the man, katana in hand. Maiya was on his other side, shivering in cold and fear, but alert. Between them, Kioko was still on her knees in the snow, her expression giving in that she was tired. Sadako had her hands on the man's arm, a trigger on her forehead, ready to be pulled. There was no way he wouldn't see any attack from them.

"What do you want?" Ayana asked. Her stubborn voice barely left her mouth.

The man had a distorted smile on his face.

"You have to come with me," he said. "You girls are wanted."

"And why is that?" she asked again.

Behind the man, shadows showed up. Slowly, the girls were surrounded by others – a total of six men. Kioko got up slowly, looking at them, her katana still on the floor so Sadako wouldn't get shot.

"Is this all necessary?" she asked. "Why didn't you guys just got into the izakaya and arrested us?"

"Why would we make such a scene in public?" the man with Sadako asked. "You geishas are our secret mission."

The men around him laughed and their laughs carried hidden intentions. Ayana had chills running down her spine. Those men wouldn't just arrest them.

"Now, put your weapons down," he said, firmly. The other men pointed their guns at them. Maiya looked at Ayana and slowly put her katana down on the snow. Ayana started doing the same, her eyes closed.

"Please," she whispered very low, to herself. She was on her knees and had her hands up. "Hina, please. Help us."

Ayana was still trying to understand her dreams. She hasn't forgotten the origamis nor the ghost, and wondered why Hina appeared for her. She needed her to appear again.

Repeating the plea for help like a prayer, Ayana felt a grip on her arms and she was lifted up. The men were taking them to a truck. They got Kioko and Maiya too, and also all of the katanas. Ayana closed her eyes and prayed again.

"Hina, tell me what you want," she whispered. "Give me a sign."

The seconds that followed were silent, as if the outside pressure had blocked Ayana's ears. She couldn't hear anything besides her breath, echoing as if she was in the inside a cave. She opened her eyes to see everything around her in slow motion – the men holding them walking as if stepping was heavy; Sadako taking forever to lower her head; the skirt of Maiya's kimono floating one centimetre at a time; Kioko's hair moving almost statically in front of her face.

Soon, the air started trembling. Ayana felt herself shaking, and a loud rustle took over. She wasn't sure if the others could feel it, but everyone seemed to see the same thing – from up in the sky, a dark cloud got closer and closer to them. Ayana was dragged quicker, hearing the men yelling commands at each other. She closed her eyes and heard them scream.

It was a brief second. When she opened her eyes again, she saw something small and dark flying right at them. Whatever it was hit the men but, for some reason, kept going right pass through her. The girls also seemed to be confused.

"What on earth is this?" the man that had Sadako yelled, losing grip of her.

"I think it's bats!" another man screamed.

Ayana opened her palm, her arm now free. Her bright skin contrasted against the dark and she could see – it weren't bats. They were butterflies. Black butterflies made of paper. And they were cutting the men.

Ayana saw that as an opportunity to fight back. That was Hina, giving her the sign she had asked for.

She turned to the man who was holding her and retrieved back her sword. Without hesitating, she swung it on him, making a cut on his chest. It was quick, but Ayana could feel how deep it was – she felt the flesh opening per her blade's soft touch, the bones cracking. The man screamed and fell. It was a smooth blow. Blood was spilled on her cheek.

She turned to her friends, who had seen the attack. Kioko

was the first one – she rushed to get her katana and made her move on the closest man, inserting the sword right through his abdomen, feeling the smoothness of his skin and the wet walls of his organs, and removing her weapon quickly. She then moved to the second man, who seemed to be going towards her, even though it was difficult. Before he could do anything, Kioko put her blade through his heart. She felt the beating stop and removed her sword, seeing a red piece of the organ on the tip of her blade. She threw it on the snow.

At that same time, Maiya attacked the man that was still holding her. Despite covering his face because of the butterflies, the man had not let go of Maiya's arm. So she turned to her weapon and removed it from his belt. Upon doing so, she cut his arm in half, feeling how easy the katana sliced his bones. The man held what was left of his limb, screaming in an agony that ended when Maiya cut his throat next, as if it were an apple she was peeling.

As soon as she had finished the first man, Ayana had moved on to the next. He had just pointed a gun at her, despite not aiming correctly because of the origami flying on his face. Ayana kicked his chest, dropping his weapon, and proceeded to cut him.

The man holding Sadako turned back to see what was happening. Before he could do anything, she got free from his grip, but didn't let go of his wrist. Upon noticing, he grabbed her own wrist that was holding his, using his strength to not let her go anywhere. Because of the effort, he fired a shot to the sky. Sadako resisted at first but, with her free arm, she reached for her katana and stabbed the man on the shoulder. He fell and Maiya rushed to finish him off before he could fire another shot at her friend. He was the last of the men to be dead.

The butterflies suddenly disappeared.

Now the girls could see the scene clearly. Their kimonos were stained with red. All six men were laying lifeless on the floor in distorted positions, the red of their blood contrasting against the snow, even in the dark.

"What... was... all... of... that," whispered Maiya, having a hard time to catch her breath.

"Whatever it was, it saved us," Sadako answered, staring at the mess they created. "But we should go. This man fired a shot. I'm sure people will be coming outside soon."

She was right. The girls ran to the truck they were supposed to be taken to. Sadako was the only one of them that could drive.

She started the car and left in a high speed. Ayana looked back to the dead soldiers and saw people had started gathering around them, confused. The girls now were far enough not to be seen by them. Even if someone saw that whoever was driving the truck did all of that mess, they would have no idea who it was.

"What do we do now?" Maiya asked, to no one in particular.

"Nothing, we will just drive to Kasai, like we planned. No stops this time," Sadako answered. "We will be safe with my parents now."

Ayana didn't like that idea.

"Sadako-senpai," she called, touching her friend's shoulder. "Whoever sent those men after us will find us anywhere. We shouldn't put your family and Koyuki-san in danger."

Sadako frowned, pressing her lips.

"So, where should we go?"

"We should continue with our mission," Ayana said. "Those black origamis were butterflies, I saw it... I asked Hina for help."

The girls didn't say anything, but looked clearly confused, demanding with their eyes for explanations. Ayana then proceeded to tell them the dream she had with her origami. Then when Hina appeared to her. And how the paper attack happened right after she called for her friend.

"I know I sound crazy," she concluded. "But this is happening. Hina wants us to achieve something, she wants us to avenge her. And this might have to do with Saito-san. She wants us to get to him by… doing what we are doing now, I guess."

She silenced herself, afraid of saying out loud they were murderers now.

"So…" Kioko started. Ayana feared she would contradict her. "Again: where do we go now? Since Hina clearly thinks we are not done. Where should we go next?"

"Osaka," Maiya replied. The girls looked at her.

Whatever innocent look Maiya had whenever she felt intimidated was gone. It was as if her eyes had gotten darker, giving her a firm, stone-like gaze. She now seemed nothing but simply tired. There was blood on her neck and hair – a blood that wasn't hers.

"Osaka is a big city, with a lot of army units," she proceeded, not looking at any of them in particular. "If we want to figure all of this out, there could be a good start."

"Well, good thing I didn't take a detour and was driving in this direction all this time, then," Sadako said, with a smile. "We are heading to Osaka already."

13

Ayana felt a smell that differed from the others she was used to. The covers in her room had the fragrance of vanilla and lilies that spread up to her window. Whenever she opened her door, the scent came to her, silent and soft, like whenever she entered Koyuki-san's office and felt the smell of peaches. It contrasted with the salty incense that perpetrated in the hallways of the house – sometimes lime, sometimes cinnamon. Scent was the first thing to be felt when one entered the okiya.

She frowned, her eyes still closed. The smell she was feeling now was sour and hot, trying to penetrate on her nose and take her breath away. It scented old, like something that was fresh when existed, but now rotted. She coughed; it was waking her up.

Ayana opened her eyes and the smell was gone, exchanged by a blow of cold air that came through the window. On her side, Maiya and Kioko were still asleep. Sadako was still driving. There were rays of sunlight coming from her, as the morning slowly showed itself. That scent could not have come from anywhere inside the truck, and the outside was nothing but a snowy road.

But she had a really bad feeling – if she didn't know how corpses smell like before, now she did. And what terrified her was *why* the idea that she felt the smell of a dead body crossed her mind.

"Are we almost there?" she asked, getting closer to Sadako, while being careful not to wake the others.

"Yes, but we will probably stop a little before, because we are out of gas. But it shouldn't be a problem."

Ayana nodded. They probably needed to get another ride from someone again.

She curled herself in a corner and waited, realizing she actually had no idea why they were even going to Osaka. Getting away from the army now seemed in vain. It would be no different from Kyoto.

She looked through the window once again. The Sun now shined brighter, getting into the vehicle. Suddenly, she saw something outside. Something shining bright, orange. It was floating, distant from her. She squeezed her eyes to see better. It was a butterfly – a real one. And soon, there were more. Ayana put her head out, seeing how they contrasted with the grey of the snow and the trees.

"Sadako-senpai," she called, getting close to her friend again. "Do you see that?"

She pointed outside. The butterflies were almost disappearing. Sadako moved her head quick.

"What is it?"

"Butterflies," Ayana responded, putting her head out the window again. They were gone.

Sadako accelerated, before coming to a full stop. Ayana quickly got back inside, Kioko and Maiya waking up. Sadako turned the vehicle off.

"We will run out of gas soon," she said. "I think we should leave the truck here and walk somewhere. I know we shouldn't be far from a place to stay."

She got out, with Ayana behind her, still looking up to the sky. The other two soon were out as well.

"Do you guys remember what Sensei said?" Kioko asked,

looking around. "I think we should practise."

The girls looked at her, not understanding. She pointed to their side, to where she was looking.

"There's a hill over there," she said. "We should go up there and train. Then we can find a place to rest."

Ayana was the first to walk up the hill. Kioko was right. They needed to bath and eat, but training should come first now, in case they ran into someone unexpectedly – like the previous night.

From the top, a village could be seen. It was clear there were houses and restaurants. Ayana smiled. They would be fine.

She looked back at her friends and saw it again – the butterflies were coming back and there were more this time. They flew by in shapes, doing curves to the left, to the right, finally arriving at the top of the girls' heads, going around them and their robes. They were surprised with that. Ayana closed her eyes. It could only be a sign again, and she wanted to feel it.

She was now sure Hina was not the only ghost around them, and that was her way of protecting the geishas.

Ayana opened her eyes again, and the butterflies were starting to fly away. They lifted from Maiya's fingers, Sadako's hair, Kioko's shoulders. The girls laughed with the tickling. They were slowly getting more and more distant, leaving behind a sense of calmness and hope.

"It looks like a sea of them," Maiya whispered. It did indeed.

The days that followed allowed the girls to keep their minds occupied. Washing their clothes and their bodies in the fresh waters of a nearby river, occasionally asking for rations, meditating for hours and training more fiercely each time gave them the preparation they needed before heading to Osaka.

When people asked, they said they were looking for their

relatives. This sympathized them with the locals – after all, an apocalyptical panic was on the way. It was easy for them to prepare their journey when they could count on people.

They slept in the truck and practised on the hill. Ayana always looked up to see if the butterflies would show up again, but they never did. Hina also didn't appear to her anymore. At first, she thought maybe she wasn't supposed to tell the others, but that soon made no sense in her mind. Now she was sure that meant they were on the right track. If they needed help, Ayana knew Hina would show up again.

ƎЖƷ

The darkness was in favour of the boys and their mothers sneaking out. The street was surprisingly quiet, making the outside even colder than usual in the absence of human warmth.

Kiyoshi made sure his mother and grandmother and Kobayashi-san were with extra layers of clothing, while he and the other two carried anything they could use as weapons – just in case. They were cold and nervous. The women never in their lives thought they would see their young children grow up in such circumstances of resorting to violence to protect themselves. Without her husband, Saito-san felt unprotected and vulnerable. Her mother was whispering a prayer.

The group walked carefully and silently for what seemed to have been hours – until they finally reached close to their destination. Yasuo turned to Kiyoshi, his long hair all tangled in itself because of the wind.

"We will go ahead," he whispered.

Kiyoshi wasn't looking at him. They were close to his home as well, after all.

He turned to his mother. Her lips were trembling.

"Okaasan," he said, holding her hands with a warm look in his eyes. "I will meet you at Kobayashi-san's place. I will be fine. We will find him."

Saito-san started to cry softly. Kiyoshi hugged her.

"I promise," he whispered and turned away, dashing to his home.

The door was already open, filling Kiyoshi's heart with hope and anxiety. He got in with loud steps, calling for his father. The house, however, was still dark as if no one was there. The only thing Kiyoshi could see was a silhouette, illuminated by the moonlight.

"Otosan?" he whispered, fearing to be wrong.

Very slowly, the man casually standing in the living room turned to face him.

He didn't reply right away. Instead, he walked a few steps in the boy's direction until he reached a full stop. Kiyoshi didn't move an inch. That was not his father.

"Are you looking for Saito-san?" the man asked.

Kiyoshi swallowed hard and, with difficulty, nodded. It was getting hard to breath.

The man took a deep breath.

"Listen… I came here because I know you were with a group of geishas, and one of them is called Ayana…"

"Where are they?" Kiyoshi asked, the words sliding out of his tongue quicker and louder than he expected. "What did you do to them? Answer me!"

The man seemed to be surprised.

"I am here because I thought *you* could answer that for *me*."

Now it was Kiyoshi's turn to be surprised, even more so than he was a minute ago. He blinked, confused.

"I know they ran away when you were all caught in this basement," the man went on. "But I haven't had any updates from them since, and my life depends on it… they are still out there, in danger because of me."

Kiyoshi opened his mouth, but he couldn't say anything. He paced around, trying to get a good look at the man's face.

"Why… what…" he stammered. "Who are you anyways?"

"My name is Taichi Imamura," the man replied. "I am Ayana's danna and…"

"So it's you," Kiyoshi grunted.

He set himself in the direction of Taichi, bringing them both to the ground. He recalled Ayana telling him about her misfortunes, and this soldier was to blame for them. He blamed Taichi for hurting the girl he loved, and he let his anger out with every punch.

Taichi dodged some of the attacks, doing his best to defend himself rather than attacking the boy. He pushed him and rolled over. He heard a grunt.

"She trusted you," Kiyoshi whispered, trying to control his breath.

"*Listen* to me," Taichi replied. He took another deep breath, adjusting himself to sit straight. "I was the one who told her about her friend and the comfort stations. I risked my life to pass this information to her, and I honestly don't know *why* they're doing what they are doing."

He took another deep breath. Kiyoshi was again surprised and attentive. Waiting.

"I told her not to do anything reckless," Taichi continued. "I thought she and the others were just worried, but now…" He let out a deep moan of frustration. "And this is all my fault. Ayana's life is at risk because of me."

Kiyoshi's mind was racing.

"And what does my father have to do with this?"

It took Taichi a second to choose his words carefully.

"Saito-san was seen going in and out of this house and, therefore, taken for investigation. It was thanks to him that those soldiers were able to burst in here and find you all hiding. Yes, the girls ran away but he had nothing do with it, and still… well, a soldier I know was injured by them. He was the one interrogating your father."

Kiyoshi couldn't find his voice.

"And?" he managed to let out a faint whisper.

"Of course Saito-san didn't have any information on him. So the soldier… well. You know what he did."

Kiyoshi released all the weight from his chest. With his face buried between his knees, he started shaking.

How was he supposed to deliver this news to his mother?

"And?" he gasped after several minutes of silence. He couldn't imagine how the situation could get any worse.

"When I found out about his identity, I came here looking for you," Taichi answered. "But now I see you are as clueless as I am." He chuckled. "It's a dead end."

Kiyoshi tried to organize his thoughts amid the sadness creeping on him. Someone killed his father. Someone killed his father and wanted to kill Ayana as well.

He couldn't let that happen.

"This soldier…" he started. "He is after them, isn't he?"

Taichi nodded, although the boy couldn't see.

"I want to get to them before he does," he replied. "You might not believe me, but… I want her safe. I want to help her, and it will be easy if we help each other."

Kiyoshi considered that for a moment. Either way, he and his friends were still following their plan.

He got up, wiping his eyes.

"We are going to Osaka," he said at last. "We can't look for them if we are stuck in a factory, and we don't want to get caught again. So we are running away."

Taichi got up in a rush, startling Kiyoshi.

"Enlist," he said, firmly. "You and the others should enlist to the army – they are going to force you to do so anyways. It will be much easier and less suspicious to find the girls if you do that."

"We know," he replied. "We will do so once we are in Osaka."

Taichi nodded again.

"Well, then… I will be going. I have to look around the city to find them before the other men do. Maybe we will meet again."

He extended his hand and, hesitantly, Kiyoshi shook it.

"Good luck," Taichi whispered, and left, going back to his truck.

With one foot heavier than the other, Kiyoshi forced himself to leave the house he wouldn't be able to call home anymore.

Ԑж3

It was finally time to go. The decision came universally, in agreement, when they saw one another's progress and knew they were finally ready. Ready to whatever waited for them in a big city, ready to whoever got in their way.

"Do you guys think Saito-san will be there?" Maiya asked. Ayana was surprised that the girl had remembered. She thought she was the only one to have worried about him this whole time.

"We can try to look for him there," Sadako said while driving. "It's very unlikely we will find him, but he might have been sent to a factory as well."

Ayana lowered her head on her knees and closed her eyes. They were also going to be sent to a factory, before all of this got out of control.

The truck's sudden stop made her wake up. She lifted her eyes to see Sadako getting out. Through the window, she could see people walking around in bicycles, cars or by foot, selling things, buying things. Ayana got out of the truck, hearing the girls behind her leaving as well. They were close to a train station, and there were a lot of people.

"What now?" Kioko asked. The girls looked around, looked at one other.

"We can try to settle," Sadako said. "We need more money anyways."

"But we can't get too comfortable," Kioko responded. "What if someone finds us again?"

"But see, Kioko-chan, those men… they could have followed us from Kyoto, but then we…" Sadako stopped, uncomfortable, cleaning her throat. "So… I think we might be safe for now. There's no way they can know we are here."

Ayana wanted to believe her, but the thrill in her body was speaking louder. Every once in a while, in a distance, she could see the military.

Sadako was walking ahead of the group, as the good leader she was born to be. She stopped in front of a store where the owner was selling grains. She bowed and politely asked him something Ayana couldn't hear. She believed her friend asked for a job, for all of them or just herself. Sadako's voice was heard again, a delicate symphony. They were out of money and needed somewhere to sleep. The man shoved them away.

There were other stops, but not much. Now Kioko and

Maiya were also worried and asking around – either for food or somewhere to stay. Ayana didn't. She saved herself the trouble to be ignored or yelled at and looked around instead, attentively. Waiting for anyone trying to take Sadako away again – or Kioko, or Maiya, or herself.

Hanako.

The cold whisper breathed itself on the hairs of her neck, giving her goosebumps. Ayana froze there, eyes wide, holding her breath. Attentive to any future callings. Snowflakes fell around her, slowly.

"Hanako-san, come back!" Ayana heard a voice urge. Her hairs got up once again. That was her geisha name.

She turned around to see two women talking. One of them was sitting down on steps while another was leaning towards her, tapping her shoulder. They were geishas.

"No way!" the one sitting said. The Hanako one. "Those men are so drunk it's impossible to do anything. You should call the others to come out."

Without realizing, Ayana slowly walked in their direction, somehow hearing the conversation amid all the noise.

The other geisha now had also sat down.

"And just leave them alone? I don't think we can do this."

Suddenly, they looked at Ayana. The girl startled, but it was obvious – she was dead staring at them. Of course they noticed.

"Oh… goodness," the Hanako geisha whispered. "Your robe is *so* exquisite." She looked at Ayana up and down.

Ayana walked a few steps ahead.

"I'm a geisha too," she said, pointing at herself. "From Kyoto."

The other two had their mouths open in surprise and looked at one another.

"Goodness!" Hanako repeated, louder. "Come here, sweetheart," she gestured for Ayana, as if she was a little kid. Ayana knelt in front of her. "What's your name?"

"Ayana," she replied, then quickly added, smiling, "My geisha name is also Hanako."

The Hanako geisha laughed, clapping her hands.

"This is awesome," she said, looking at the other one. "They can call her by the same name!"

She then turned to Ayana.

"We are having the hardest time entertaining some men because a few of them are so wasted and we really want to go home," she said, as emphasizing her speech and facial expressions, sighing, as if her job was tiring her a lot. "It would be *so* great if you could cover it for us, Ayana-chan… you can even have some of the money."

Hanako winked, teasing. Ayana's eyes opened wide.

"I have to tell my friends…" she said, looking around. She saw Kioko was looking straight at her. Ayana waved, calling her. Meanwhile, the geisha asked the other one to call the girls that were inside.

"Listen," she said, turning Ayana to face her. "They are some businessmen doing heaven knows what," Hanako rolled her eyes. Soon, the other girl returned, bringing three more with her. There were loud voices coming from inside. "Just sit there for a little hour until they get kicked out or something, okay?" Hanako then smiled and patted Ayana on the shoulder. "Let's go girls!" she called the others and they went ahead to get a cab.

Ayana felt a gentle poke. It was Sadako.

"What was that?" she asked, looking over to the geishas.

Ayana turned to her friends with a smile.

"An easy way to get some money," she said, and started

walking to the teahouse, the others behind her, intrigued. "You will see."

As soon as Ayana opened the door, she was face to face with the moustache of a man. His hair fell down his face and his shirt was unbuttoned, revealing a tanned chest. He looked at her up and down. The smell of alcohol came from his nose.

"What… oh!" he yelled, smiling. Ayana tasted beer. "Look at this!" He turned to the others. "Something better came in!"

The men laughed and applauded, loud, saying things that were incoherent. The one at the door pulled Ayana in and then the others. The girls looked at one another.

"Let's do this," Sadako whispered. She then turned to the men with a pleasant smile and sat on the floor, in between two of them. "How are you gentlemen doing today?"

She poured them more drinks. The first man grabbed Ayana by the waist, his face really close to hers.

"Why don't you sit next to me, beautiful?" he whispered in her ear. Ayana was disgusted, but went ahead with it.

She sat on the floor next to that man, who poured her a drink she didn't accept. Kioko and Maiya now were also sitting, in different corners of the table. The men were talking about whatever superficial things they were talking before, but the girls did not have a chance to engage in it yet, only Sadako. Ayana always thought she was the most professional of them.

At that moment, while trying to focus on what the people were saying, Ayana looked around for clues to talk to them and get her money. Then her eyes locked with one of the guests, who seemed to have left somewhere and just gotten back. He had a green uniform on, a camouflage.

He looked at the scene, hesitating as if he was surprised, and left again, before anyone even noticed him. Ayana kept staring at where he came from. Later, in minutes that seemed like forever, he returned, looking at each of them with a stern expression.

Ayana's heart started beating fast and loud. She looked over at Sadako, who seemed aware of the man's presence. The girl stood up at the invite of another guest, sitting next to the soldier. Ayana really wanted to know what the two of them were talking. She looked for Kioko and Maiya, seeing the other two were also tense.

Shortly after, Sadako got up, serious, discreetly looking at the girls with urgency. She walked through the door the soldier came from, and he was right behind her. Whatever they whispered about did not end well, and only confirmed the girls' fears.

Some men saw the two of them and made dirty jokes, but Ayana couldn't pay attention anymore. She got free from the moustache man's arms, right when he was about to kiss her, and stood up, leaving through the same door at the same time as Kioko and Maiya. They heard the men protesting.

In the hallway, Sadako was pinning the soldier against the wall, her sword on his neck.

"How many?" she asked.

The man laughed.

"How many minutes? How many men? Why does it matter? You'll all be dead anyways."

Sadako touched his nose with hers.

"And so will you," she whispered, slicing his throat. The man sled down on the wall, grunting, with his left hand holding his neck. Sadako looked at the others and turned to continue to run down the hall. They followed her, while the man struggled to live his final moments. They didn't wait for him to end, they didn't wait to make sure his life was gone. They didn't have time for grief or guilt, and weren't impressed by death anymore.

Sadako saw a door at the dead end of the place and sled it open. It gave access to a salon decorated with big paintings on the walls and shelves full of china, red walls with columns and a mirrored floor. That was probably used for very special occasions – weddings, anniversaries, important meetings. There were sets of stairs on each corner, leading to what seemed to be another hallway with more doors, but the girls couldn't see clearly, as they only looked up very quickly. The place seemed to be empty, each step they took creating a loud echo.

"We could hide here," Maiya whispered, not wanting her voice to be an intruder. She looked up and started walking towards the stairs. "We could go up there."

"Shhh! Maybe we're not alone," Kioko replied.

"And you're absolutely right," a loud male voice said. The girls turned around, scared.

The vast room was now packed with men in their uniforms. Ayana was alert, her heart beating as fast as ever. The adrenaline was taking over all of them. Again, Ayana felt the rotten smell of a corpse. She frowned.

The soldiers slowly walked to keep themselves around the girls, in a circle, as if they had no rush in doing anything. The geishas slowly took their katanas out, standing in position. Sadako's sword still had the soldier's blood in it. The drips fell constantly.

Some of the men laughed.

"This won't work," said the man who had spoken to them first. He gestured for one of his guys with his head, who walked forward.

Ayana saw him ready to get his pistol out, when Kioko dashed to him, screaming, her katana up. She cut his hand, the blade passing through the skin, veins, flesh and bones, creating layers as it opened each of them. The hand fell with the fingers still holding the gun. The man was mute, looking down at his arm, saliva dropping from his open, perplexed mouth. Kioko put her blade right through it. The man fell, his eyes rolled up, turned white. He froze in a forever expression of shock and fear.

Ayana held her breath, waiting for the worse. There were a dozen of them, at least. They all seemed surprise with such agility Kioko had acquired. The soldier who seemed to be in command had his forehead frowned, shocked. He had fear in his eyes.

Nervously, he gestured for another man, in an awkward way, with his hand shaking at no one in particular. One of his subordinates took his gun and pointed it at Kioko. Considering what she had just done, it wasn't a smart move. She dodged. The bullet hit one of the windows, the glass shattering like rain.

Kioko moved further, crouching down before the man could fire another bullet. But she went straight to the boss, embracing him in the stomach and making him fall with her weight. It was all very fast. He pinned her down and she kept resisting, both of them involved in a fist fight.

"Go get them!" he yelled, startling his men.

It was time to run again.

Ayana went to the place she thought was most logical – the stairs. She started going up the steps, men behind her. She saw Maiya was doing the same, on the other side, men after her as well. Sadako stayed to stop more men from going after them. Surrounded by four soldiers, she flipped her katana around like it was a rope. She stuck her sword in the chest of one of them, who got too close. Another one grabbed her arms. She started to throw herself from side to side and back and forth, still fumbling her katana around.

At that moment, Kioko ran towards her, leaving behind the commander with his face down and a puddle of blood under him. The men with Sadako looked at Kioko's direction, to the mess she did. They had no commands anymore.

Ayana reached for a door, seeing Maiya was still on the other side. Both of them had divided the group. She heard shots being fired and squeezed her eyes, hoping it didn't get her friends.

She opened one of the doors that lead to a bedroom. The cream coloured walls contrasted with the dark floor that matched more paintings hanging around. On one side of the room, there was a small wooden shelf composed of drawers, and a mirror. On the other, a window. In the middle, a carpet and a large bed.

She stood behind the door and closed it as soon as the first man entered the room, locking it. He turned around, face to face with the girl who held his arms and turned them, standing behind him. Fires were shot through the heavy door, and Ayana used the man as a shield. She let go of his body and it made a loud thud. There was silence. Breathing fast, she looked around to see what could be done, but was out of options. She couldn't hide or leave. Using her katana was the only way.

The door opened aggressively, but the men didn't fire – they couldn't risk killing their friend. So, Ayana used that moment to behead the first one that showed up. It took her less than a second, she didn't even see it coming – it was automatic, as if the sword had gotten longer, as if it had a life of its own.

The only soldier left didn't let surprise take him for longer. Grunting, he ran in Ayana's direction and threw himself at her, making her fall on the bed. He was holding her wrists and, therefore, her blade too. He pinned her down on her hips with his knees, sitting on top of her. She couldn't move.

Maiya ran up as fast as she could, seeing Kioko and Sadako struggling downstairs, and Ayana on her left. Perhaps the two of them could meet once they got upstairs and fight together. But then she saw that Ayana ran into one room. So she ran into one as well.

Once she opened the first door, the men after her were still going up the steps. They couldn't exactly see where she was. She noticed the room was full of paintings, with a bed in the middle. It had a certain European style to it, with heavy, dark furniture and furry carpets. But she didn't have time to admire it. She just ran towards another door within that bedroom – it led to a bigger room, like a common area. There was a big chandelier on the ceiling, illuminating the place with its lights and crystals. Right under it was a big green and golden table surrounded by matching chairs and, in the middle of the table, a big white jar with pink flowers.

Several shots were fired. Startled, Maiya ran towards the jar and picked it up, running in the direction of the furniture. She hid inside a closet, praying that her friends were alive.

There were muffed voices outside, and Maiya held her breath, squeezing her eyes shut. The men were nearby and could find her if they looked around well. She peeked outside and saw the three of them were walking around the room, shouting at one another. They knew there was where she went, and knew she couldn't have gone anywhere else.

Maiya backed off from the door as much as she could. Carefully placing her katana next to her, she held the flower jar with both hands and raised them. She heard steps coming closer.

As soon as the door opened, she used all her force in her impact to throw the jar on the man's face. The ceramic broke on his skull, opening deep scratches on his forehead, eyes, nose and lips. The men yelled, water, sand and flowers falling on him. Maiya got her sword and finished him off.

Right then the other soldier pointed his gun at her, but she dodged any possible shot, moving her katana like it was a part of her. She kicked the man on the chest, knocking him off his balance. That gave her the opportunity to cut him. She felt it was a difficult, heavy cut that took her what seemed to be forever to finish but, suddenly, she had done it. After a minor struggle, her blade slid down and she felt the hardness of the floor.

The last opponent came back from wherever he was, taking a brief second to process what he saw. He couldn't believe how such a small girl could do so much damage to two grown men. But, looking at her, he understood – her face had an expression he had never seen in anyone in a long time. It was the face of someone who gave up on everything, and had nothing to lose.

Maiya roared at him, adrenaline rushing inside her. He was in front of one of the chairs. It was the perfect location. She aimed her sword up and threw it at the chandelier as if it was a boomerang.

Kioko sat on top of the commander, finally pinning his wrists with her feet. He could still grab her ankles, but it wouldn't do much. She stuck her sword right through his throat and got up right away, blood on her robe, running to Sadako, who had just stabbed someone. One of the men held her arms. Kioko went for him, but was stopped by another soldier, putting himself between her and Sadako. He held her katana with his hand, making Kioko kneel slowly, with her back bent backwards. She looked to the side and saw a third man getting his pistol, ready to shoot Sadako.

Kioko then threw herself at the man in front of her, while Sadako herself twisted and turned around. Kioko rolled over, getting rid of the man's grip and positioned herself on her knees again, putting her katana in front of Sadako while kicking the soldier right when he was about to fire.

His shots went up to the air, after one hit his fellow colleague and another one hit Sadako. The soldier holding her fell, lifelessly, while she grunted. There was a wound on her lower side.

Shortly after, a very loud crashing sound interrupted them, startling everyone.

Upon the startlement, Ayana used that moment of distraction to cut the head of the soldier on top of her, the blade going right through his soft throat. Ayana got up with blood on her face and neck, and ran to the stairs. She looked to her side and saw Maiya running as well, realizing her friend had caused that loud sound of millions of glasses falling.

When they both got downstairs, the last two men were quicker. One of them got up, pinning Kioko down. The other one had his arms around an injured, weak Sadako.

"Drop your swords," said the man holding her, between teeth. "Or we will finish her off."

"We have orders to bring you all, dead or alive," completed the other man, struggling a bit with Kioko. "So cooperate."

Ayana's mind was racing, but she still held tight to her weapon. Maiya, on the other hand, let go of hers.

"Drop your sword!" the first man yelled again. "Reinforcements are coming. You have no chance. Now, *drop it*!"

Ayana did as told, raising her hands up. She looked at Sadako. Her friend was breathing with difficulty, eyes closed. She needed help urgently.

At that moment, a loud grunt was heard from behind the men, in a dark corner. It was gravelly and low, like an animal. The soldiers turned around to see a girl wearing a dress that was covered in blood, her skin dark with rot.

The girl walked towards them slowly, back curved and knees bent, with her mouth open and blood coming out of it. Her grunting didn't stop. Ayana felt a warm liquid run down her legs.

It was Hina. An ugly, sombre version of Hina.

The soldiers muttered nonsense, eyes wide, legs shaking. They let go of Kioko and Sadako, who fell on the floor.

"G…. ghost, *ghost*!" one of them managed to say, while the other stumbled when trying to get away. They both ran. Whoever they were going to, had to believe in them. After all, two people cannot see the same paranormal things at the same time. Telling what happened also meant they would prove not to have been able to complete their mission.

Hina turned her attention back to the girls. Although none of them had taken her eyes off her, she was suddenly different. In the blink of an eye, she looked like she always did – no blood, no wounds. Just her pretty face, her braided hair.

She knelt next to a horrified Sadako.

"Shhh," Hina whispered. She held Sadako's shoulders and leaned the girl on her, pressing on her wound. "Breathe in and out slowly, darling," she said, her once strong accent almost completely gone.

Sadako did as told, without taking her eyes off her friend. Kioko slowly crawled towards them, not believing her own eyes. Maiya was crying. Ayana's vision was blurry with tears. Hina had never showed up to all of them before.

The door opened and more men came in. The girls turned their attention to them right away, out of habit. There weren't as many this time, but the girls had no strength to fight again.

"What…" one of the men whispered, getting closer to them.

He seemed the one in charge there. He stopped right in front of Maiya.

"Oniisan," she whispered.

It was her brother. It had been years since they last met.

"Did you… kill all of them?" he asked her, whispering. His eyes were wide open.

"Two escaped," she answered in the same way. They were both very similar to one another – the same innocent eyes.

He held his breath, visibly nervous, and looked around.

"Your friend needs care," he whispered. The girls looked back to Sadako, who was now lying on the floor. Hina was gone. "Go."

"W… what…" Maiya whispered again, slowly getting up, not believing what was happening.

"I said," her brother repeated, louder, but still only they were able to hear. "Go. Get out of here. Now."

Slowly, Kioko put Sadako on her back. Ayana got all four katanas and touched Maiya's shoulder.

"Let's go, honey," she whispered. The other men close to them were as confused and horrified, but did not dare to move. The girls had to take their chance and leave.

Maiya held her brother's hand while being taken away.

"Oniisan," she called, louder this time. "Oniisan, please… don't."

With difficulty, he let go of her hand and looked away.

Maiya was now screaming and crying, calling for her brother by his name, while Ayana, carrying all the swords, tried her best to drag the girl with her. Kioko was already ahead of them with Sadako, going back to the teahouse's corridor. Once Ayana and Maiya also got out of the room, they started to run, before any more men went after them. The entire place was now empty.

The girls dashed to the populated street, attracting some looks. There was no way they would not call anyone's attention – Sadako bled and Maiya sobbed uncontrollably, knowing her brother's life had ended. He risked himself to save her own life, after years of not hearing any news from her.

They had gone too far and there was no going back now.

14

The fishermen's tales say they come at night, moving as if they were part of the shadows, their steps smooth like silk.

Rumours say they float in the air.

In the light, they mix within the crowd. In the darkness, they blend in.

Any trooper walking alone is the perfect prey.

Especially those who whistle. Ghosts are called that way.

When you least expect it, they take your breath with a cold, shining touch.

Your throat is slit, your heart is poked out, your head is pinned. Silently.

No witnesses. No evidences.

Villagers say they are spirits looking for vengeance. Beautiful girls in disguise.

They came because the war is upon. They revenge the children of the overseas.

They will beg you for money and beg you for food. They will dance for you and they will seduce you. But be no fool. Do not give in to their charm. Do not fall for their entertainment. Do not let their words get to your ears and their smiles get to your heart.

They will serve you a tea as warm as their touch, play the shamisen as if the strings were your feelings, pour the sake that will drown you into unconsciousness.

They are not humans, but sirens with swords for tails.

So beware, soldier!

For if you fall for their magic, your uniform will be the only thing left of your honour.

ƐЖЗ

The excited voices of the people intertwined themselves with the smells of food and perfumes. The night sky shined with fireworks and the streets were illuminated by stalls and lanterns along the river.

Ayana felt free to go out unnoticed – in a dark yukata and a kitsune mask, she knew she wasn't to be seen by anyone but her friends.

Maiya was busy buying sweets while Kioko and Sadako looked at white lanterns hanging from the sky.

"The boats are probably looking so gorgeous right now, with the bonfires," Kioko exclaimed. "We should go see it!"

Once Maiya returned and handed them food, the girls started walking towards the river. Ayana followed them, eating her chocolate very slowly, savouring every sweet moment. That was the one little bit of peace they could get amid everything that was going on. She knew it wouldn't take long.

She was tense, however. Those years were years of blind patriotism and pride. Uniforms were seen everywhere and flags of the empire hang in the air, a line of white and red curtains.

Ayana shivered constantly. That same ideology was what killed her friend.

And every progress they made seemed to not be enough. Ayana looked around her and saw so many victims – she could easily sneak behind a stall and slip the soldier's throat. Or stab the one that just passed through her. She could have pretended to bump into him by accident…

Ayana shook her head. That was always on her mind – the annihilation. She couldn't stop fearing for her friends' lives or her own; she couldn't stop thinking they could be found at any moment like they were found before. There always seemed to have coincidences happening around them; signs. As if they were always receiving some guidance.

"Are you okay, Ayana-chan?"

Ayana looked over to Sadako. She was done eating her dessert.

"I…" Ayana started mumbling, noticing she was the only one who didn't eat everything. "Yeah! Just looking at the fireworks," she replied and proceeded to eat and feel the sugar in her tongue with every bite, contrasting with the bitterness of her life.

Kioko placed herself in front of them, forming a circle.

"Let's go to the riverbed," she whispered, looking dead serious and adjusting her mask. That was their signal when trouble seemed to be near.

The others dressed the white foxes in their faces and walked along, heads down. There wasn't a moment of peace.

The girls gathered themselves in a corner of a stall, near a boat, where some people talked. The spot wasn't illuminated much, giving the geishas the opportunity to study their surroundings better. Ayana could see there was a bit of an unusual movement – they got used to see these things: the rush, the loud commands.

"I will go up there to see better," Maiya said. The girls looked over at her as she was climbing some wooden boxes at the back of another stall. They all walked over there, now completely invisible in the dark, where their kimonos felt at home.

They climbed the boxes one after the other, going up the walls and then the roofs. Ayana could see the colourful crowd in their orange, black, pink and blue attires, holding red paper lights and dancing. The fireworks illuminated the sky in white, green, purple, red.

Amid that rainbow of faces and fabrics, Ayana could see soldiers walking on opposite directions from the crowd or talking to one another while looking around. When a firework popped, the girls crawled to hide themselves so as to not be seen.

Maiya walked slowly, laying down, to the tip of the roof. Standing low, she placed her foot at the tip of a tile and jumped, smashing her arms and fists in the tiles of the other roof, soon pulling her body up and standing. She signalled for the others to follow her.

Kioko held a scream both when Maiya tried to jump and when she herself did so. Ayana went next, struggling less than the others due to her height. Her legs swung in the air, not touching anything. For a brief second, she felt adrenaline rushing over her veins.

Sadako hesitated for a long time, pressing her hand against the place where she got hit by a bullet.

"You can do it," Ayana whispered, extending her arms. Both Kioko and Maiya were alert, positioning themselves so that they could hold Sadako in case she fell.

At last, the girl jumped. With one arm stretched, she grabbed onto Ayana, who fell, holding herself on the tiles with her other free hand. Kioko and Maiya grabbed her legs.

The girls grunted, trying to pull Sadako up. Her body was hurting.

"You can do it," Ayana whispered again, with difficulty,

while pulled her friend up.

Slowly, Sadako laid on the tiles, praying she hasn't been noticed.

"What now?" she asked.

Kioko was already looking ahead.

"I think we will need to jump more roofs."

The girls looked over to the crowd. More soldiers were being gathered around the area.

Perhaps they have been seen after all.

"They seem to be a bit lost," Kioko said. "But still... how can they spot us?"

"A really good eye did," Ayana said. She has had enough of this chasing.

Walking over to the end of the roof, she hesitated to create impulse before jumping again. A tile cracked and fell, smashing on the dusty ground. She walked over to the edge that faced the crowd.

People in their yukatas seemed cheerful in that summer's Tenjin Matsuri, despite the current situation they were at. From afar, Ayana could see the Noh play on the floating stage while fireworks popped.

"We really should stop with this," she heard Sadako complain. "My scar still hurts."

Ayana turned to look at her friend and put her hand on the girl's shoulder.

"I think we are safe for now," she said.

Run.

Ayana shivered with that delicate whisper. It was familiar.

And it meant something bad was about to happen.

She glanced up at the street right away. At that instant, she saw a man on top of a roof in the opposite direction. There were others climbing behind him. He had a gun.

They weren't safe.

"Down!"

Ayana screamed, pulling two of the girls, all of them laying on the tiles, while the bullet whistled on top of their heads. Their feet were slippery and more tiles fell on the floor.

Sadako slipped on the tiles, her silky dress sliding down as she went with it, screaming. Maiya threw herself to hold her friend's arm.

"Sadako-senpai!" Ayana called and, just as she was about help Maiya, Sadako fell.

The girls screamed, going over to the edge, only to see Sadako being held by three men. She didn't fall, they had pulled her.

Kioko jumped, landing on one of the men, who grunted when his body hit the floor. Kioko pressed him there, with her legs on his shoulders. Before he could reach for his gun, she cut his face in half and got up at that same second, going for the other man.

Maiya and Ayana also had jumped, kicking the man that held Sadako, before rolling on the grass. Sadako struggled with two men before her friends had knocked one of them out. She took her sword out, engraving it in the soldier's neck. He gasped and held the blade, blood dropping from his red hands.

From behind him, another blade popped out, going right through his chest. The man's expression froze in big round eyes and a bloody mouth. Sadako removed her blade while the other was also removed, and the man fell. Ayana was the one at his other end.

The third man laid on the grass, with his lifeless body covered in cuts and dressed in nothing but stripes. Kioko and

Maiya had gone in circles, swinging their swords around him.

Ayana looked in the direction of the boats.

"We should try to go to the river," she warned the others. "Others will soon find us here."

Slowly, they got out from behind the dark and, with their masks on, made their way through the people, their katanas hidden against their skins.

Walking to the docks, it was possible to see they wouldn't be able to simply hop in on a boat, as they were all occupied by people and had limited space. They were also in the middle of the water already.

So Ayana decided to go there.

Crouching down, she sat on the dock, putting her feet in the cold water. The chill went over all of her body and she held her breath, getting in.

When she emerged, the girls looked confused.

"This is the only way we can hide," she said. "We can even clean ourselves."

Kioko shrugged and jumped. Maiya helped a hesitant Sadako slowly sit on the floor before diving.

While the blood washed itself away, dissolving in the dark water, the girls started swimming to the boats. At a fair distance, the men on the boats saw them, surprised. Ayana put her mask up, showing her face and smiled, waving at them. The young ones started laughing, the excitement of seeing girls their age in wet dresses making them blush. One by one, the geishas got in.

"We want to have some fun," Ayana giggled, making some of the men giggle too.

"But it's *so* cold," Maiya cried, holding herself onto one of the boys and faking a shiver. He gladly took a blanket and wrapped it on her shoulders.

Ayana looked around, alert to any possible threats while overhearing her friends laugh and lie about why they were on a boat. They never had to try hard – only pretend they were drunk or very extroverted.

Men were always easily bewitched.

Several minutes passed, and the girls were well camouflaged into the group of men on the boat. The public mainly focused on the bonfires, and no one seemed to mind their presence. Ayana let herself relax, feeling the water brush against the tip of her toes.

Until a hand grabbed her ankle, pulling her out of the boat.

Ayana only had time to gasp softly before falling in the water in a matter of seconds. She emerged, ready to scream when a hand covered her mouth. A soldier was swimming behind her, holding her with one arm and trying to reach the deck with the other. Ayana violently moved her arms and legs, splashing water. She tried to call her friends, but the man was too strong, although he also struggled.

Sadako was the first one to notice what was happening. She went over to tell Kioko and Maiya, being careful not to call any more attention. When Ayana realised, she was being lifted up.

"Sakura-chan, what were you doing there?" the man that dragged her out of the boat said, a theatrical tone in his voice.

Ayana was confused, but not stupid – that man was wearing a uniform. There were a lot of people there, and some looked over at them, curious to why he jumped in the water to take her out of a boat.

"Did you drink again? Otosan is going to be very angry," he said, wrapping his arms around her and walking away with her.

Ayana did not try to resist. She simply looked behind and saw the girls were on the other margin, staring at her. She knew they were thinking of a way to get to her soon.

"Sir, please let me go," Ayana whispered, trying to sound scared. "I don't know…"

"Shut up," the man said, with a stern expression and a hispid voice.

Ayana tried to resist, seeing that now there weren't people around them anymore. The soldier kept hugging her tighter, forcing her to walk along with him. She started kicking him and turning. He fell and brought her along.

"Enough," someone said. An authoritarian voice.

Ayana froze and the man stood up right away. She looked up to see an older man, staring down at her. There were other two men with him.

Slowly, Ayana stood up, without taking her eyes off him.

In a subtle move, she took her katana out, turning around and placing it on the neck of the man who brought her there. Before she could do anything, she heard the other two take their guns out.

"Don't try anything," the older man said.

She had her eyes locked on the soldier in front of her. He seemed angry but scared. His hand was placed on his gun, still in his belt. His breath was fast and loud. The adrenaline could be felt in the centimetres separating the two of them.

Ayana was about to back off when she heard quick, soft steps. The man took his eyes away from her to look behind her. His pupils dilated and his mouth opened in slight shock. Ayana knew what it was.

Without hesitating, she sliced his throat.

When she turned around, the old man was still there, seemingly unsurprised. Behind him, the other two men were replaced by Kioko and Maiya, while their lifeless bodies laid on the blood-covered floor. Sadako caught up to them.

"Impressive," said the old man, ignoring the swords the girls pointed at him. "Exactly what I was expecting."

"Who are you?" Ayana asked. "What do you want?"

"I should be the one to ask these questions," the old man said. He took a few steps further, getting closer to Ayana. She positioned her sword up. "Why are you girls doing this?"

"How dare you have the audacity to ask," Sadako was heard. She had a very deep voice when situations escalated. It was easy to pay attention to her.

The old man turned around with one arched brow.

"We lost a dear friend because of you," she continued. "We found out what is happening in Manchuria. We are forcing a war we will lose. Why?"

"Friend?"

"Yes," Ayana said, the old man turning back to her. "She was in your comfort stations."

Ayana walked closer to him.

"Why do this?" she asked, genuinely curious. She was tired.

The girls closed themselves in a circle, coming closer and closer to the old man. He was getting more and more uncomfortable.

They started interrogating, wording out every question mark they had. Every doubt, every frustration, every anger they had carried for months.

For each different outburst, they stabbed the man. His inability to keep up with the girls' fast-thinking and retaliate rewarded him his first cut, right in the arm. From there on, the girls swung their katanas around, brushing them against his now red uniform, until he too, fell.

Hanzou stood there, seeing Kaito Nakamura covered in blood, surrounded by a group of women who had lost hope. A group of women that, while wiping their tears and catching their breaths, managed to create chaos. They mobilized numerous men to stop them, started a silent revolution and created discomfort in people. They were tired of the thirst for power that men had.

Whatever supernatural force walked alongside those geishas, it sure gave such power to them.

"The stories are true after all," he whispered.

The four geishas looked at him, not realizing they were not alone. There was a brief second of shock in the air.

The tension was broken when one of them started laughing, walking in his direction. He knew what was coming for him. And he deserved it.

With watery and angry eyes, Kioko raised her katana.

15

Yoshiki sat next to Kiyoshi.

"Do you think the stories are real?"

Kiyoshi knew what he was talking about. He knew his friend's brother also couldn't stop thinking about it.

"Part of me wants to believe it isn't," he answered, lowering his head. His fingers were busy with a stick.

Yasuo was inside a store, getting some food. Since they moved to Osaka, they had enlisted on the army. Their decision of running away from the factory nearby Kyoto was good only because they never wanted to have gone to one in the first place. But the bad side was that they could never imagine the degree of the situation getting any worse.

When Kiyoshi went to Yasuo and Yoshiki's house on the night he met Ayana's danna, he could barely contain himself. As if no words were needed, his mother threw himself at him in a tight hug and they both mourned. No one was able to sleep after that.

Kiyoshi's grandmother didn't have all that energy anymore – to run for her life, to eat almost nothing. She went to sleep one night and never woke up. But he was not sad. His mother also wasn't. Although they were still mourning, they knew it would be better for her to finally rest.

And the girls. They were also looking for them.

"Well," Yoshiki said. "Part of me wants to believe it is. That means they are alive."

Kiyoshi threw the stick on the floor.

"That also means they changed, for the worse," he replied. "That's why part of me wants to believe it's all rumours."

He started walking away. Yoshiki followed him.

"But rumours do start because of some sort of evidence, and there has been plenty…"

"Which proves my point," Kiyoshi snapped. He looked at his friend with a sad expression. "I'm sorry, Yoshiki-senpai. I just don't want to picture Ayana…" He shook his head.

Yoshiki put his hand on Kiyoshi's shoulder and squeezed it.

"We knew this day would come eventually," he said. "They told us their story and we helped them. Wouldn't you be happy to know they live?"

Kiyoshi knew his friend actually meant Ayana, rather than all of them together. He also knew, deep down, that was the truth. He wanted them to be alive. He wanted *her* to be alive.

"Yes, of course," he said, letting a big sigh escape.

Yoshiki tapped his arm.

"Let's go meet Yasuo," he said. "And let's not give up yet – not now that we know they are here in Osaka, too."

Kiyoshi nodded.

"Let's not."

He walked in just in time to help Yasuo carry the food. Every time they went out somewhere, Kiyoshi looked for a familiar face. He always hoped to see Ayana in the crowd, waving at him and smiling, telling him all of this was over.

And, every time, he asked himself if he would be able to even recognize her.

After all, they haven't seen each other in years.

꒰Ж꒱

"Years!" Kyo yelled, his arms up. "It has been *years*."

His room was packed with his men. They were all confined in rolls next to each other, firm posture with heads down, ashamed. Kyo paced around, breathing loud. Sweating.

"Years passed and I still don't have those geishas with me!"

The only noise in the room was from a fan, swinging around, not being able to cool down the temperature.

Kyo put his hands on his desk.

"Yamamoto and Nakamura are gone. Our activities are no secret to the public anymore," he whispered. "And we are losing the war... we are a weak country."

He looked up to his subordinates.

"I am sure none of you want this shame on yourselves. They are no mafia, no organized crime. But their influence sure is big, and damages our reputation as an empire."

He emphasized the last word, backing away from his desk and staring at his men, one by one. Until he stopped in one of them.

"Imamura-kun," he called, a firm voice.

Hesitantly, Taichi stepped in front.

"Sir," he whispered.

Kyo got closer to him.

"Word of mouth says they are still in Osaka, so go get them," he ordered. "Clean up the mess you made, like I had ordered you to. Your life depends on it."

"Hai, sir," Taichi answered, trying his best not to seem nervous.

On that same day, he got off the train, stepping into the station. He was in Osaka, at last.

He knew it wasn't going to be easy. The men he met had ideas of where the girls had been and where they could go next, but none of them wanted to be sure. Taichi knew, deep down, that they were afraid of the geishas – and too ashamed to admit it.

He understood them. He had also heard the stories.

But he wanted to help the girls as well. Since meeting Saito-san's son, Taichi had relentlessly looked for the girls in neighbouring areas, hoping destiny would put him and Hanako together. He wasn't afraid of her – he knew he could find her and not have the need to run away.

With the rumours of them being in Osaka, he did his best to avoid having to go there, hoping they could hide better. Hoping he wouldn't have to meet them and end their lives – but also eager to see Hanako's face once again.

Taichi soon found himself in a bit of a crowded street, close to some buildings that were serving as improvised clinics for the injured ones. Everybody seemed to walk in the same direction, so he just followed them for a while, often ending up at dead ends or desert places and going to where he originally was, to start again.

At one moment, he felt a very cold and small hand grab his, sending a chill over his entire body. He thought it was a lost child and turned around quickly, not seeing anyone. In fact, he was all alone.

And then, he saw her.

At the very other side of the narrow street he was at, Taichi saw a group of girls walking straight, but not in his direction. They were fast, their dark robes swinging at the bottom, heads low. Hanako was there, her hair tied up in a tall bun. She seemed to be in a hurry.

He started running to them and opened his mouth to call for

her. But before he did so, he saw a group of men on their other side. They were soldiers. They were after the girls.

Taichi ran faster. And, while doing so, he loaded his gun.

ϾӜЗ

The bombings happened sometime in the summer.

Ayana wasn't going to lie to herself anymore – she saw it as a sign the empire was crumbling. That made her happy – it meant their revenge on Hina was working, not only by their own effort, but also by destiny.

She knew they were on the right track because Hina hadn't showed up since that night at the teahouse. Many times, Ayana closed her eyes before sleeping, fearing she would see that gruesome scene again, the grunting and the blood. She would then regret it right away. Hina would never haunt her.

Still, a fight like that one hadn't happened since. The girls practised every morning, hiding in a forest, or in the middle of a field. Or at the silent night of a city, when its habitants were in their homes or the secluded shelters.

Ayana would always hide in those, hoping to see Kiyoshi running along the people, with fear from the missiles, hoping to crouch on a safe space underground. But, whenever she looked around or stayed behind, the only familiar faces belonged to the girls; her friends, her sisters.

Temples were somewhere she would go often. She wanted a sign from Hina. She wanted to know where Kiyoshi was, if his family was alive, if his father was found. The girls were looking for them. They would protect themselves on the way, from possible predators – it was for precaution.

They almost lost their lives so many times already. They

couldn't take the risk.

Anywhere they went, despair went along. The people were hungry, scared and cold, running from explosions because their lives, for the first time, depended on their speed and energy. The girls had it – years had passed since they were on the run, after all. But not everyone was as lucky.

That was the sad part for Ayana – they were losing the war, and the people were the ones to suffer the most.

When the faint morning came once again, everyone got out of the shelters, only to see the destruction outside. People walked stumbling, as if they were infants taking their first steps. It was always like that. It was always hard to stand up, hard to open your eyes. It was hard to see your home shattered.

They passed through what once was a complex of houses, a narrow neighbourhood that was now nothing but a pile of dust, wood and bricks. People either ran in a rush to get somewhere, or in tears, or walked like them – in silence, in emptiness. There were burned corpses on the floor.

As if drawn by curiosity, Sadako entered one of the buildings. A lot of people were walking that way, to start. One by one, the girls got inside of what used to be a school. It was full of people, most of them sick. Nurses ran around with their white aprons stained in red like paintings. On the floor, people moaned in pain, laying on thin mattresses, covered in gauze and blood.

"What a chaos," Maiya whispered. She started walking around.

Kioko was horrified by what she saw, walking on her own direction. She saw children crying, teenagers missing a leg or an arm – or both. They looked dirty, the bandages looked old. War was an ugly landscape.

"H… hey," a faint whisper said. The voice was nearby and

very weak. It grabbed her hand.

Kioko quickly turned around, only to see a man with messy hair, a head bandage and the face stained in red and brown. He was lying next to a woman, full of gauze.

"Kioko," the man whispered.

The girl's eyes flooded with tears as she slowly knelt next to them. They were barely recognizable. But Kioko remembered them well.

She remembered the days he arrived home, drunk. He would beat her, but it was never his fault. It was always the alcohol.

She also remembered her leaving. She said she couldn't take it and, the next morning, she was gone. Left her alone with him. A little girl and a drunk man.

Kioko had no idea how they were together again. But she was certain that, if this meant something, it could only be fate.

"You grew so much," the woman managed to say, amid coughs. "We… watched you dance… you looked so beautiful."

Kioko's tears were now rolling down her cheeks, nonstop. She was controlling herself not to sob.

"Does it hurt?" she asked, her voice cracking. The man started crying, nodding.

Kioko didn't know what to do, but she couldn't let them suffer that way. Whatever happened in the past didn't matter in that moment anymore.

She looked around to make sure no one was seeing her. Whipping off her tears, she got up and knelt again, in between the two of them.

"Don't worry, it will stop hurting now, all right?" she said, with a tender voice. Both of them nodded, faintly.

Discreetly, she took her katana out, resting it low on the floor for nobody to see. She took the man's head, lifting it and he rested it on her chest, his back facing her. Kioko acted as if she was adjusting his bandages. She then put the katana through, the tip of the blade showing on his abdomen. He gasped softly. Kioko removed the blade and laid him down again. She turned to the woman, who was sobbing, trying her best to keep her voice low. She grabbed Kioko's hand and sat down with difficulty. She then opened her arms, for a hug. And the two of them hugged, crying. Soon, the woman stopped, and Kioko removed the blade from her flesh. Crying by herself.

She put their mattresses closer. They both looked peaceful, immersed in a deep sleep. Kioko said a prayer.

"Otosan, okaasan," she whispered. "Goodbye."

She got up and recomposed herself, walking to the nearest exit.

"Kioko-chan?" Ayana called her. "What happened?"

Kioko turned to the girls, but didn't look them in the eyes.

"Nothing, I'm fine," she whispered. "Let's just get out of here."

The girls walked after her and turned in a street. There weren't many people in there, and it was getting dark. They would have to find a place to sleep soon.

Sadako saw, with the corner of her eye, some shadows. They weren't exactly dark, but not near enough for her to distinguish forms. They walked behind columns on the other side of the houses.

She hurried her step.

"I think we are being followed," she whispered.

The girls lowered their heads and walked faster as well. There was no one around and no sounds nearby now. Anywhere they turned, they would be alone.

Soon, they heard a shot being fired, the bullet hitting

somewhere near, startling the girls. They screamed.

"This way," Sadako said, and they started running to yet another street, while shots continued to be fired. The bullets passed right through Ayana's ears, in a high-pitched buzz.

Maiya was the fastest one. She reached for a door first, of what seemed to be of an abandoned house. It was not completely destroyed, but the front door was locked. She then walked around the place, looking for other doors, and found a way in, the girls following her.

Still, they kept running around the neighbourhood, among the houses and the wreckage. The men were not far from them. Ayana could hear their steps getting closer. They could hit them for real at any second now.

A lot of shots were fired, one after the other. The girls screamed and ran even faster. They looked at one another, realizing they were all fine, and came to a stop. The men were dead.

"What was that?" Kioko asked, whispering, in between breaths, with her hands on her knees.

"Hanako-chan!"

Ayana turned around to see who called for her. The voice was familiar, like a voice she had known during childhood, of someone she knew and missed, that now came back from the dead.

It was Taichi.

He looked anxious, eyes open wide, while holding Ayana's elbow. As if he was waiting for her to recognize him.

Ayana asked herself what he was doing there, until she realised that was the only explanation. It was because of him they could escape.

"You helped us," she said, surprised. "But… why?"

"Why wouldn't I?" he replied, taking a deep breath and letting the air go. "I am too involved with you to let this slide. I needed to see for myself if you were okay."

Ayana frowned.

"What do you mean?"

Taichi looked over to the others. His eyes showed disturbance and anguish.

"The reason why they are after you is because of the letter I sent," he said. "They figured it all out, and now Akemi Ito and his men are after you... I'm sorry. I was an idiot."

Ayana looked over to her friends, but they also looked confused, not seeming to know what he was talking about. She turned her attention back to Taichi.

"You did what you had to do," she said, giving him an awkward smile. "But who is..."

Before she could complete her sentence, a shot was fired. They all froze in place, hearts stopping, breaths being held.

"It's him," Taichi whispered. "Run!"

He started pulling Ayana by her elbow, the girls running behind them. They dodged from other bullets while new sets of steps were running after them. The little houses were soon replaced by trees that grew taller and bushes that grew thicker. They were entering a forest.

Taichi had let go of Ayana's elbow and was running next to her. The other girls were sprinting on each side of her – everyone seemed to be in sync.

"Imamura-senpai!"

The voice behind them called, hispid and loud.

"Who is that?" Ayana yelled, looking at Taichi.

"Akemi Ito," he replied amid his loud breath. "He's after you!"

Another shot was fired somewhere and the girls flinched. Akemi did not seem to be after anyone in particular, making all the geishas his target.

"You should leave them alone, Imamura-senpai!" Akemi yelled again. "Traitor! What are you trying to achieve?"

This time, Taichi was the one who turned around to fire a shot. Akemi laughed in response, sounding like a maniac.

In a fast manner, Ayana put herself behind a tree. As the group was spread out and Akemi was alone, it would be difficult for him to figure out where exactly she was.

As if noticing something was missing, Taichi hid as well, shortly after Ayana. The girls did the same, one by one, metres apart.

Akemi came to an abrupt stop, looking around anxiously, his gun up. He started walking around the trees, looking for his victims. Ayana held her breath, hoping he wouldn't find her friends.

She saw Kioko going after him, katana in hand. She dashed to her friend, trying to be as silent as possible. She heard someone behind her.

From her left, she saw Taichi come out from behind his hiding place and fire against Akemi, with no luck. He turned towards the sound, being face to face with his opponent. The girls were parallel to them, observing from afar.

Taichi didn't raise his gun, although he was alert to any sudden movements. Akemi grunted and turned to run away, looking back and firing another shot.

It was all very fast.

Soon, a red stain started to form on Taichi's uniform, moving slowly, like the tentacles of an octopus. He looked down at himself and knelt, Ayana kneeling with him. She heard the girls gasping.

"Hanako-chan... I'm sorry," Taichi whispered, letting the rest of his body fall to the ground.

Ayana held his head.

"Shhh... don't say anything," she replied, pressing her hand against his wound. She was looking at him, nervously. It was the first time she was fearing for Taichi's life.

"I never appreciated you," he continued, ignoring her plead. "I used you and, for a while, I didn't care," he coughed, blood coming out of his mouth.

"Taichi, stop!" Ayana cried, pressing against his wound even harder.

"The things I was doing... it was just so you would leave me alone sooner, but... I now realise I wanted to keep you around... I wanted you often, but wasn't man enough," he cough again. "Forgive me."

He looked her in the eyes. They were wet and shining. She never saw him crying, never saw any emotion despite annoyance on him before.

And now, there he was. A little boy. A scared little boy.

Ayana opened and closed her mouth, looking for words.

"Of course," it came out. "We can talk after, but I need you to be quiet for now."

Sadako was knelt next to her, overlooking his situation to figure out what to do. Maiya and Kioko were in front of them, protecting them.

On the other side, Akemi had a smile of satisfaction on his face.

"Hana...ko...chan," Taichi whispered. Ayana turned her attention back at him. Sadako was improvising a first-aid care on his torso. He held Sadako's hand, although his eyes were on

Ayana. "There's no use… I will be with our baby soon," he coughed. "I actually really want them to be a girl… because she would be pretty like you," he laughed, softly. Ayana did the same, caressing his hair. She felt tears starting to form.

Taichi's expression turned sad again. He touched Ayana's cheek.

"I never knew… who you were," he whispered. "What is your… name?"

Ayana was ready to answer when, suddenly, Taichi's finger dropped, no longer caressing her face. His eyes turned to the side, as if he was looking at nothing in particular; as if they were empty.

Ayana's body started shaking as more tears came out. She started sobbing.

"It's Ayana!" she yelled, shaking Taichi's body. "My name is Ayana! Please, Taichi, come back! You have to hear it, please! I'm Ayana…"

He was gone.

She felt arms around her. It was Sadako, pulling her gently for a hug.

"Shhh…calm down," the girl whispered, rocking her back and forth softly, while Ayana had her head down, repeating her name over and over in whispers that became weaker each time she spoke. Taichi needed to hear her.

A loud laugh echoed. An evil laugh, that made Ayana freeze. A laugh that took Taichi's life.

"Traitor!" Akemi screamed, laughing again. "Tell me, *Ayana*, do you want your revenge? Do you want to fight me and make me pay for what I did to him? Do you want to slowly put your sword through my heart and twist its blade and feel my muscles and hear me scream?" he paused, pacing around. He moved his arms while talking, in an exaggerated way. "*Do you want that?*"

Ayana did not answer. He started walking towards a field, as the trees started to disperse.

"I will be right over there," he said, leaving.

For several seconds that seemed to go by very slowly, the girls didn't move. They didn't know what to do.

But Ayana's blood was boiling. She could feel the heat going up in her body, her cheeks were red and sweat started to form on her face. She hated that man.

Getting free from Sadako's arms, Ayana reached for her katana and dashed to the field.

16

Akemi was standing straight, looking at the horizon. Ayana came up to him slowly, hesitantly. He seemed to be contemplating the view with nostalgia, almost as if he was a sane person. The Sun was rising and its shy light touched his white skin, enhancing a long scar he had on his cheek.

He started to unbutton his uniform, as if he had no rush to do anything. No rush to kill or to die. Like nothing mattered to him anymore and he had not a single thing to worry about.

His bare back revealed he had even more scars – a pattern of thin reliefs in coral colour that could be vividly seen on his pale body. He turned around, facing Ayana, and she could see more scars on him, but one stood out the most – the one Kioko created on his chest, deep and dark. That scar screamed at Ayana as if it wanted to be seen. As if *he* wanted her to realise how dangerous all of this was.

Akemi smiled.

"Do you remember this day?" he asked her, pointing at his scar. "Probably not, right? You were not the artist."

He was referring to Kioko. Ayana looked over to where her friends were. She could see the top of their heads and their katanas too, moving.

"Don't bother," Akemi said, his eyes still fixed on her. "I brought some men to keep them busy. But this," he walked closer. "It's just between you and me."

Ayana frowned.

"Why? I didn't hurt you."

Akemi looked at her as if he didn't understand her, and then proceeded to laugh. He laughed like she had said the best joke he ever heard.

"Ayana-chan… you were the most involved in this. Imamura-senpai told the secret to you and no one else."

He walked closer to her, removing his belt and the guns that came with it.

"I like a fair game," he whispered slowly, dropping the belt. "And, as you can see, I don't mind scars either."

He positioned himself straight, hands closed, pressed against each other. Ayana stood leaned forward, her right leg stretched behind while her left knee was bent. She held her katana tightly, fixing her eyes on Akemi. Again, Ayana felt the strong rotten smell she was now familiar with, and frowned. Those were probably, the corpses of the soldiers that made Akemi's company. Bad spirits that surrounded him.

She felt the top of her head tickling and looked up discreetly. A few butterflies were flying, not far from her. It wasn't a big group like she had seen before – she counted three. But that didn't matter. She knew Hina was there for her.

Ayana closed her eyes and took a deep breath, feeling the place around her. Whether she lived or not, she had to take him down no matter what.

She opened her eyes again, and he had on his face a creepy smile; a winner smile. An expression that showed he would end her no matter what, as well.

Then, he sprinted.

She turned around and started running, startled.

"Running away so soon?" he yelled at her and laughed.

The truth was that Ayana figured that going towards him

could cause her katana to crash on herself instead. She needed impulse if she wanted to target him right. But nonetheless, that fight was the one with the least sense to her. She didn't know what to expect.

They ran far, to the point where Ayana would look back and not see her friends anymore. The hill had ended, but Ayana kept running down and stopped at the beach. There was nobody around. The wind was strong, blowing on her hair and bringing the salty smell of the water. The waves crashed on the sand like an aquatic thunder. Gulls could be heard and a navy ship could be seen, at a far distance.

Ayana made a turn as soon as she saw trees. Hoping to hide herself among the tall trunks, she sprinted further and further from the sand.

An arm grabbed her abruptly and she fell, soon being lifted up again.

An old man had his hand tightened around her elbow. He looked at her as if she was a disgusting insect he wanted to step on.

"You come with me," he grunted, dragging her to the left.

Ayana put her katana back where it belonged. The old man had a gun pointed at her.

Kyo held the girl with difficulty, despite noticing she was collaborating with him and not resisting. He shouldn't have sent Taichi there alone. Because of him, that boy was dead.

He let go of her arm.

"Why did you kill him?" he asked, again in a deep voice.

Ayana hesitated, scared. Who was he talking about? Akemi wasn't dead.

Kyo took a deep breath.

"Imamura-kun."

Ayana's vision got blurry.

"I didn't," she managed to say. "I wanted to save him."

"So it was true after all," he said with a sad smile. "He did help you."

Ayana started crying. She was the one who had dragged Taichi into that mess. He was dead because of her, and now it was her turn to die.

Kyo crouched down in front of her. She felt a pistol on her head.

"I have men taking care of your friends for me, as the two of us talk now," he said. "I like a fair game."

"Unlike me, right?" she whispered. Kyo hesitated to answer.

Ayana figured that, if she was going to die in that instant, she could say whatever was on her mind without fear.

"You implied I don't like a fair game," she said, louder, a smile on her face. "But, you see... I killed many men because they killed many women."

She looked at him with hate. Tears were fallen from her eyes.

He was one out of the many rocks life was throwing at her. And she was tired of breaking them.

"So tell me... how is this not fair?"

For the second Kyo Watanabe processed the question and thought of an answer, Ayana stood up while getting her katana out in lightspeed. A shot was heard. He had pulled the trigger, hitting a tree.

Right at that moment, she beheaded him.

Someone started clapping. Ayana turned around to see Akemi.

"That was..." he started. "Fast. Precise. Monotone too. Honestly? A little lame."

He slowly walked in her direction.

"I like to hear the screams and see the blood… it gives more adrenaline, don't you think?"

Ayana started backing off, holding her sword firmly.

The faster he walked towards her, the faster she got away.

☧Ж3

Dust fell down from the ceiling once again. Kiyoshi closed his eyes shut while his mother squeezed his arm and the shelter shook.

"I have to go now, okaasan," he whispered after a while.

"Please, be careful," Saito-san whispered. He left her and Kobayashi-san alone, and went outside to meet Yasuo and Yoshiki. The brothers had aged considerably, with hairs on their cheeks and worry on their eyes. He knew he had aged as well. There was no way, in those circumstances, that someone wouldn't lose a few years of their lives.

They were also tired. With untidy uniforms and constant fear for their lives, they had not given up on the geishas. They patrolled and followed whatever orders were given in the hopes of finding the girls somewhere by unknowingly taking part on the secret mission of going after them, to no avail.

The posters might have stopped long ago, but stories had started to form and were persisting along with many other urban legends that surfaced thanks to the war. In the chaos of it all, it was difficult to know what was true and what wasn't – and if the girls were still alive.

Once Kiyoshi was standing very close to the other two, he raised his brows, waiting for updates.

"Ito-senpai and other men are here on orders from Watanabe-san," Yasuo informed. "It seems they have found a lead on the girls."

Kiyoshi's heart started racing. He took a deep breath, trying to find words.

"How come?" he asked, frowning.

"That man, Imamura-senpai, was sent here. They know the girls are here."

"We think," Yoshiki continued. "That, if we find any of them, we can find the girls as well. They were spotted nearby!"

Kiyoshi nodded, looking around anxiously. Yasuo started running ahead of him and so, he followed his friend.

They got inside a truck and drove to nowhere in particular. If the girls were indeed here, they wouldn't have to look much, but they still had to be faster than their enemies – the other soldiers and Akemi Ito.

Yasuo was able to spot an odd movement, stopping the vehicle abruptly. All three of them got out in a rush, running towards another group of soldiers that had their weapons ready. The boys caught up to the others and kept running, hoping it would lead them to Imamura-senpai eventually.

"They are over there!" a soldier yelled, pointing ahead of them.

And indeed, much ahead of where they were located, amid tall trunks of trees, Kiyoshi and the brothers saw shining swords swinging in the air, and they couldn't believe their eyes.

ꙥЖꙅ

Akemi did not seem tired, unlike Ayana, who was breathing as fast as ever. She occasionally turned around to face him, swinging her katana in the air in a clumsy way, in hopes he would back off and stay distant from her. He would take a couple of steps back or tilt to one side, but never lose his pace or take his gaze off Ayana.

The girl had her eyes open wide, gasping and feeling tears about to come out. She feared that man more then she had feared any other she had to fight against. All of them were predictable killing machines. But that one... he was the total opposite. Mad. She just wanted to get away from him.

And, in that desperation, she tripped. Falling on her back, the soft sand felt like concrete. The air escaped from her lungs.

Akemi jumped on her. His knees held her legs, and his hand held her wrists. Not being able to get a hold of her katana, she kept grunting, trying to move and shaking her head repeatedly, to avoid his eyes.

"You have nowhere to run now," he whispered on her ear, biting her lobe softly and moving his lips to her neck. Ayana was disgusted.

He laughed.

"I am the winner," he said, an ugly smile on his face. "I will live."

He lifted one of Ayana's arms and moved it closer to the other. Ayana noticed a slight struggle on his fingers, as he was trying to hold both her wrists with one hand. But, once he let go of that one arm for a brief second, Ayana saw her chance right then. With all the strength she could gather at that moment, she slapped his cheek. Akemi grunted, surprised, and Ayana turned around to run away again.

Without getting up just yet, she crawled from under his grip as fast as she could, using her elbows and forearms one in front of the other on the sand, to stay as away from him as possible.

Akemi grabbed her ankle and pulled her to him. Standing, he grabbed her arms and put her back on her feet.

"I am the one in command!" he yelled in her face. "You will do everything I say!"

He threw her back on the sand, and Ayana hit her face in it, scratching her left cheek and the side of her eye, now burning. Akemi was on his knees again, holding both her arms. He was too close. That was her chance. She couldn't move in any other way.

So she bit his face.

Akemi screamed inside her mouth, while Ayana pressed her teeth on his jaw. He let go of her arms and held her neck, backing away. Ayana put her hands on his arms, coughing. He was choking her.

"Stay still or I kill you!" he yelled, his chin covered in blood.

In an impulse, she grabbed a handful of sand, throwing it on his face. He screamed, reaching for his eyes. Ayana kicked him on his rib and backed off, getting up.

She ran to her katana, grabbing it the moment Akemi got a hold of her by the hips, lifting her up. Her katana fell again.

He ran with her to the water and threw her on the sand again, in the moment a small wave had just broken, its white foam hitting her face. He then lifted her up, only to throw her in the deeper water. Ayana was swallowing all the salt, choking and gasping for air.

Without any coordination, she fell multiple times on her own. Akemi turned her to face him, putting his hands on her neck once again. Keeping her immersed. Ayana kicked and punched, to no avail.

Until it finally worked. Everything was quiet.

She opened her eyes. She wasn't drowning. There were no waves around her. No Akemi.

Ayana was floating in the middle of an immensity of blue.

Shy rays of sunlight illuminated the space. Ayana could see her kimono lifting slowly and her hair spread out. Bubbles came out of her mouth.

She was in the middle of the ocean.

She closed her eyes, accepting that was it. Akemi had let go of her and the waters had welcomed her in.

Why did you leave him? Hina had asked.

"You didn't leave me, Ayana-chan," a familiar voice whispered. An echo. "I was the one who left you."

It was Taichi.

That voice was his.

All that time, Hina was talking about him.

Ayana opened her eyes. There was something coming towards her. She looked at the shape, trying to focus on it. It came slowly and paced, becoming clearer each second that passed.

It was Hina.

She touched Ayana's left cheek, looking at her with tenderness.

"There's one more thing for you to do," the girl whispered, her voice reverberating across the space.

She looked down and Ayana looked down with her. Something at the very bottom of the ocean was shining, going up, closer to her. It was her katana. It floated slowly, stopping once it reached between the two girls.

Ayana held it on her open palms and looked back at Hina. Her friend winked and disappeared, bubbles surging where she was before.

The bubbles were coming from the bottom as well, but in a speed that created a current. Ayana's body was trembling with the vibrations.

She then found herself surrounded by orange butterflies.

Hundreds of them. They swirled around her legs, hips and hair, going up. Showing her the way out. Carrying her to the surface.

Ayana opened her eyes. The salt made it difficult, but she could definitely see – Akemi was above the water, his hands on her neck. She had only one hand holding him. The other held her sword.

A force lifted her up, bringing air to her face again. She was not controlling her movements. Akemi had a confused look, surprised by how fast and sudden she had gotten up.

Then, she sliced his neck.

Ayana fell on her knees, gasping and coughing. With the corner of her eye, she saw a tall figure standing next to her.

It was Kiyoshi's father.

"Saito-san…" Ayana whispered.

Saito-san crouched in front of her, a tender and calm expression on his face.

"Don't worry about me, child," he said. "I never left any of you."

He touched her face and Ayana suddenly knew – Kiyoshi's father was the one who moved her katana. He was the one who killed Akemi. He got his revenge.

And disappeared along with the wind.

Ayana got up with difficulty, slowly walking to the dry sand. Now, she just had to go back to where she ran from. She could see foreign ships and flags at a distance.

There were blurred shapes running towards her. Their screams were muffed. Ayana put her katana high in front of her, but fell on her knees with the effort. Arms grabbed her.

"Ayana-chan!" a voice called. "Look at me!"

Her face was being held. That allowed Ayana to focus her vision. It was Kiyoshi. His toned skin was stained with dirt and sweat. His hair was long and thick, and his beard had grown. He had aged. But still looked like the same Kiyoshi Ayana remembered.

She touched his cheeks and his head, not believing in what she was seeing.

"You're alive," she heard herself whisper. Kiyoshi nodded.

She kissed his lips and hugged him.

"You're alive," she whispered.

He was also hugging her, rocking her body against his.

"I am, and I will never leave you again," he whispered back. "I promise."

Ayana started crying. She soon felt other hands on them. Kiyoshi lifted her up with him, still holding tight to her.

She saw all of her friends. They were covered in blood and dirt. They were hurt. They were tired. But they were alive.

Ayana started laughing.

"You're alive," she repeated, louder. "We are alive!"

Sadako hugged her first. Soon, the others had their arms around them.

"We did it," she whispered.

Kioko now was laughing too.

"We did it!" she screamed excitedly, hugging the girls again. "I can't believe we did it!"

"We can go home now," Maiya said, while they broke free once again. They could see soldiers from abroad nearby.

Ayana looked at each one of them, as the realization slowly fell upon the group.

The war was over.

17

Sadako didn't even turn the truck off properly when she jumped out of it and ran in the direction of her house.

"Okaasan! Otosan!" she yelled, going down a grassy hill. The girls followed behind her, walking slowly.

In a distance, a woman sled the main door open and smiled. She ran and hugged Sadako. When the girls caught up to them, a man was also hugging the girl. They all exchanged words and how they were glad to be safe and sound.

"Where is Koyuki-san?" Sadako asked, getting in the house and looking around.

Ayana noticed a gloomy expression on the faces of her parents. She looked over to Maiya and Kioko. They both noticed it as well. The three of them hugged, in silence.

Sadako came back to the living room, confused. She wasn't seeing the woman anywhere. And why were her friends looking so sad?

"Okaasan… where is she?" she asked in a deep voice, expecting the worst.

Silently, Sadako's mother went over to one of the side tables in their living room and picked a jar up. The porcelain shined and had light green and blue colours in it, making wave patterns. It was a tall jar with golden details. The lid had a little ball on top, also in gold. Sadako opened it, but felt stupid in doing so. She closed the jar and hugged it.

"How?" she asked, in a whisper. Her eyes were blurry.

"Heart attack," her mother replied.

Sadako fell on her knees and cried. Koyuki-san had raised her.

Ayana went over to her friend and knelt next to her, putting her arms around the girl and letting her rest her head. A shoulder to cry on. The other two slowly did the same and soon, all four of them were embracing one another.

The mix of feelings felt like a storm. Ayana was grateful for having everyone alive, except... the most important person for them. She could feel a cold wind down her spine, as if the clouds were whistling another set of rain. She wondered when the Sun would show up again.

A few days had passed until Sadako finally decided to go back to Kyoto. They were all feeling slightly better. Koyuki-san wouldn't have wanted them to grieve for longer and leave work behind. The war was over and it was time to get back to business, she would have said.

"We need to take advantage of the time the Americans will be spending here," Sadako told her mother. The girls were organizing the truck. "I promise I will visit more often."

They hugged their goodbyes and Sadako walked over to the truck, ready to drive. For a brief second, she stopped, hesitating, and went to hug her parents again.

"Thank you for taking care of her," she cried. Ayana went over to her and held her by the shoulders.

"Let's go, darling," she whispered. She bowed to Matsumoto-san and they got in the car. The girls waved goodbyes to Sadako's family until they couldn't be seen anymore.

Ayana held Koyuki-san's ashes during the whole ride.

The looks people gave the geishas were noticeable – they

knew who they were, at last. But everyone was too busy trying to move on with their own lives to make any accusations or ask any questions. The streets were a fuss and different faces were seen everywhere – foreigner hairs and foreigner eyes.

The girls stopped at the entrance of the okiya, holding their breaths. They were about to unveil old memories from a time that seemed to have been from long ago. Ayana held firmly to the jar, the same way she had always held firmly to Koyuki-san's hand.

She felt someone gently touching her shoulder and turned around. It was Kiyoshi.

He smiled, but his attention soon turned to her hands. Ayana looked down, her expression turning sad.

"Heart attack," she whispered.

"I'm sorry," he whispered back. He then looked at the door. "I see you guys are ready to get in."

The girls looked back at the door. Sadako turned the key in.

"All right," she whispered, and opened the place.

The front yard was full of leaves and water ran out of a tap on the floor. They went to the backyard, and that wasn't much better – the trees needed to be trimmed. The grass was tall. The bath house was dry, covered in leaves and dust. The whole place needed urgent maintenance.

The inside, however, didn't seem much changed, except for all of the empty rooms and, of course, the dust. It was easy to see it floating on the golden light of the Sun, as if they were snowflakes. Ayana went to her room, seeing the girls were each going to their respective bedrooms as well. Everything was exactly the way she left – her makeup carefully closed on top of her table; her bed done with the same red cushion she had put there; her drawers organized; some clothes on a chair. She closed her eyes and felt the smell of lilies. For a moment, she forgot everything that happened. Like it all had been a terrible nightmare.

But the weight on her arms remembered her otherwise. Still, she looked down at the jar and wished things could go back to the way they were.

Leaving her room, she went to Koyuki-san's office. Sadako was standing there already, looking around at what was now her own office.

Ayana carefully placed the jar at the table. The whole room was still organized, just like the woman had left it. Still smelling like peaches. She expected Koyuki-san to come through the door behind them at any second now. But, as much as they waited in an anxious silence, nothing happened. The woman's sense of presence was so strong and yet, she was nowhere to be seen.

"We could plant her," Sadako said. "Turn her into a tree."

Ayana looked at her friend. That was a good idea.

"Then we need to clean this whole place first," she said. "That's what she would have wanted."

A light knock made them turn around. It was Kiyoshi.

"I can ask for help," he said. "You will need to fix a lot of things around here."

Sadako bowed.

"Thank you, Kiyoshi-kun."

He nodded and left. Maiya and Kioko were right behind him, and entered the office as soon as he left. They both got closer to the table.

"I will miss her," Maiya whispered, tears forming in her eyes.

Kioko sobbed softly.

"When we saw those injured people back in Osaka... I saw my parents."

The girls turned their full attention to her, surprised. But none dared to say anything.

"I… killed them," Kioko whispered, almost without voice. "They asked me to… all this time…" She sighed with a weak voice. "I only had Koyuki-san with me. And now she's gone, too."

She started crying softly. Maiya hugged her. She could relate to that. She lost her brother.

Slowly, one by one, all four of them hugged, all together in the sorrow of loss. The losses they suffered and the losses they caused.

Sadako was the first one to break free.

"We have each other," she said, standing in front of the other three. "We can do this and we will do it, for Koyuki-san," she looked at the jar. "She's watching over us."

Ayana looked up to the sky, through the window. The sun was clear, illuminating the room. A thin light in all that darkness.

"All of them are," she whispered, not needing to give further explanations.

ƸӜƷ

Ayana lit the incense next to Hina's picture. The photos she had given to each one of the geishas were placed one next to the other – her house photo, given to Ayana; a photo she took of Maiya standing next to flowers; one of her and a laughing Kioko; and her own smiling face, a photo given to Sadako, placed right in the centre of the altar that was set up for her.

The girls never found out the real name of their dear friend. She never told them because she was told to choose a Japanese name to be included in society. Now, Ayana understood Hina was forced to do so. Just like she was forced to do many other terrible things in order to survive.

As time passed, the geishas found out, with the help of Kiyoshi and the brothers and a few of Taichi's fellow soldiers, that there were way more comfort stations and comfort women than they could have imagined – hundreds of facilities spread out across the continent with thousands and thousands of women in them – although they never seemed to find an exact number.

Some were even located in cities across Japan. The girls regretted not having knowledge of them so early, as it would have been much easier to invade those establishments. They could have saved those women from the abuse and the negligence of their freedom.

Perhaps, by doing so, hundreds of thousands of those women would have been alive now – including Hina. She most likely lived in terrible conditions in a place like that, having to endure pain coming from several men every day. Ayana shivered. She and her friends might have decided to put an end to their vengeance once the war ended – but she knew that fight would still go on in the decades to come. She knew Hina's neighbour and all those who had survived still had a long way to go. And she was certain Hina had not survived because her willingness to escape had costed her life – and not only hers, but of many others.

"Hina," Ayana whispered, tears falling down her cheeks, a faint smile on her lips. She gently raised her hand to caress her friend's photograph. "You brave, brave girl," Ayana chuckled. She was sure each one of those women had a lot of courage in them.

"May your soul rest in peace, sister."

EPILOGUE

The faint light of the Sun opens my eyes. I stare back at it. It's spring.

I make my way through the busy hallways of the okiya, where little girls run to their daily classes, the geishas get ready for their errands and the maids prepare our breakfast. The fragrance of sakuras fills the air.

Their petals are everywhere in the garden, where I go water her. She is shy now, still growing, her plants still small. The peaches will come in time.

I kneel to smooth the soil when an orange butterfly lands on my palm. It goes up in the sky while I look at it getting closer to the others. They fly around the flowers and around me. The sea of butterflies.

I watch those souls drift away and whisper a prayer.

Sayonara.

THE END

ƸӜƷ

Dear reader,

Thank you for coming this far on my story – I sincerely hope you have enjoyed it. It has been a long time since I was able to come up with something that I'd want to write and, when the idea for this book first came to me in the Summer of 2019, I knew fate would help me publish it.

Well, here it is: not just the idea but the theme I used as a background inspiration. I have noticed a quite limited market when it comes to the topic of geishas and so, when investing in this theme, I relied on History to provide me with an interesting filling on how my story would go and how my characters would grow.

The research I made consisted of watching interviews, reading articles and gathering some opinions. I recognize the topic is a very sensitive one, and that is exactly why I chose it, given so many people don't know about it.

My goal with this book is not to point fingers at anyone, but show how we all share a common ground and certain degrees of suffering, anguish and sadness. After all, there is no winner in a war when lives are lost.

Therefore, dear reader, I hope you have appreciated this book and all the work put into it. It is my first published work of this extent in the English language, and I believe some people will find it enjoyable.

Bruna.